★

"Mine!" Nicole poured on the steam, her eye on the ball.

The dark-haired Asteroid appeared. She was shoulder-to-shoulder with Nicole. They battled for control.

Nicole tried to focus on the ball. Her frustration was rising. Why couldn't this chick let her get off one clean shot?

The Asteroid reached out and started to draw the ball away.

"No!" Nicole yelled.

The Asteroid took control of the ball. She turned her shoulder to Nicole. Another second and she'd boot the ball out of reach.

A good sport would accept the fact that the Asteroid was a better player. Nicole thought about her mom saying *she* was a good sport. Well, now Nicole could prove that her mother didn't know anything.

Nicole pulled back and kicked the Asteroid in the knee.

Teaming Up

Teaming Up

by

Emily Costello

A SKYLARK BOOK

NEW YORK · TORONTO · LONDON · SYDNEY · AUCKLAND

RL 5, 008–012

TEAMING UP

A Bantam Skylark Book/May 1999

Skylark Books is a registered trademark of Bantam Books, a division of Random House, Inc. Registered in U.S. Patent and Trademark Office and elsewhere.

ISBN 0-553-48684-5

Published simultaneously in the United States and Canada

Bantam Books are published by Bantam Books, a division of Random House, Inc. Its trademark, consisting of the words "Bantam Books" and the portrayal of a rooster, is Registered in U.S. Patent and Trademark Office and in other countries. Marca Registrada. Bantam Books, 1540 Broadway, New York, New York 10036.

PRINTED IN THE UNITED STATES OF AMERICA

OPM   0   9   8   7   6   5   4   3   2   1

For Mason and Claire

chapter 1

"THIS ONE IS MINE!" NICOLE PHILIPS-SMITH called. A second later the soccer ball crashed into her chest. The impact knocked the breath out of her.

Nicole shook it off and sprang into motion. The ball bounced a few feet. She raced after it, got control, and dribbled toward the Asteroids' goal.

As she ran, Nicole read the field. Two Asteroids were covering Tess Adams, who was playing right attacker. Kyoto Funaki was still pounding up the left side of the field. Nobody was in position to help.

"Tie it up!" Lacey Essex called from the sidelines.

Don't worry, Nicole thought. The Stars—her American Youth Soccer Organization team—

were behind by one goal. She was determined to change that.

She pushed herself to run even faster. The gap between her and the goal shrank. The Asteroid goalkeeper was hovering near the left side of the goal.

Nicole chose a spot to aim for: up high, on the right side of the goal. Just a few more feet and she'd be in position to shoot.

"Asteroid alert!" someone shouted.

"Behind you, Nicole!"

Nicole glanced back. She caught a glimpse of dark hair. In the next instant the Asteroid was right up next to her, pushing against her right shoulder and reaching for the ball with her left foot. The Asteroid was short, but fast and tough. She'd been on Nicole's tail for the whole game.

The girls battled for the ball. Nicole saw a blur of cleats, grass, knees. She tried to keep her eye on the ball.

"Get it, sweetie!"

Even in the middle of fighting for the ball, Nicole recognized that voice. She glanced toward the sidelines. Her mother smiled and waved.

Seeing her on the sidelines was weird. Before

that afternoon, Nicole's mom had never come to her soccer games. But Ms. Smith had decided to make some changes in her life. And making time to attend Nicole's games was part of her plan.

Nicole looked back at the ball—just in time to see the Asteroid draw it away from her. Nicole reached way out with her right foot. She slipped and landed hard on her bottom. The Asteroid whacked the ball back toward the halfway line.

Tess ran over. "Are you okay?"

Nicole scrambled to her feet, brushing herself off. "Yes, yes. Come on! Let's get the ball."

"Fine with me!" Tess hurried back toward play.

The Asteroids dominated play for the next ten minutes. Tess finally regained control of the ball— about two seconds before the ref signaled halftime.

Nicole groaned in frustration. She started toward the sidelines.

Geena Di Gregorio ran up and fell into step beside her.

"You looked good out there," Geena said.

Nicole rolled her eyes. "Scoring would have been nice."

"True."

"Every time I got close to the goal that same stupid Asteroid stole the ball," Nicole said. "My mother is ruining my concentration. She starts shouting every time I get near the ball."

"Well, I wouldn't call it *shouting*," Geena said. "It's more like *cheering*."

"Whatever it is, she's making too much noise," Nicole said. "Why can't she respect the fact that I'm trying to concentrate?"

"Nicole!" Geena laughed. "It's not like we're playing chess."

The girls had reached the sidelines. They headed toward the team's big water cooler and poured drinks for themselves.

Nicole downed her water in one gulp. "Why is she interested in soccer all of a sudden?"

"She probably thinks you like having her here." Geena's voice was soft.

Nicole rolled her eyes. That comment just proved how little Geena knew about her mom. "Trust me," Nicole said. "My happiness has nothing to do with this. Mom never considers how I feel."

"Mr. Thomas, may I make an announcement?" Tess asked the Stars' coach during the break. "It's about soccer."

4

"Okay, Tess. If you can get their attention, you can talk to them."

"Good luck," Mrs. Essex, the Stars' assistant coach, said. "They're half asleep."

The team did look tired. They were playing a tough game. But maybe Tess's news would inspire them.

She climbed up on the team's aluminum bench. "Hey, everyone!" she called. "Could I have your attention for a minute? I have an important announcement to make!"

She waited until all ten of her teammates were looking at her. "I discovered something amazing on the Internet last night," she announced. "The U.S. Women's National Soccer Team is going to play in Chicago next month!" Chicago was only about half an hour away from the girls' hometown of Beachside, Michigan.

"The women?" Sheila McGarth asked.

"Of course the women!" Tess beamed just thinking about them. Forget Mark McGwire and Michael Jordan. To Tess, the members of the U.S. Women's National Soccer Team were the best athletes in the country. If not the world!

Tess especially loved the attackers. She was

dazzled by Mia Hamm's intensity and aggressiveness. Tess had met the great forward at a tournament earlier in the season, and she'd been impressed by how down-to-earth Mia seemed.

And Michelle Akers . . . Tess had just read a book about her performance at the first Women's World Championship in 1991. She'd scored an incredible ten goals during that tournament. The United States never would have won the title without her.

Tess was just as excited to see the younger forwards. It wasn't hard to imagine some of them still playing ten years from now. And that meant Tess might just get to play with them. Her plans definitely included a starting position on the U.S. Team.

"Are you going to go?" Yardley Gallagher asked.

Tess nodded vigorously. "I wouldn't miss it. But I have an even better idea. What if *all* of us go together? I'll organize the whole thing—find out how much tickets cost, get some parents to drive us down, collect the money—everything!"

"Sounds great," Tameka Thomas said.

Kyoto nodded. "Those chicks are my *heroes*."

"I think my mom would drive," Yasmine Madrigal added.

Nicole raised a hand. "Just one thing," she said. Tess looked at her. "Yeah?"

"Make sure you get good seats," Nicole said. "The last time I went to Soldier Field it was a waste of time. We sat way up high, and I couldn't see a thing."

"Sure," Tess agreed easily. Good seats, bad seats—it was all the same to her. She just wanted to see the women play. Maybe they could even wait after the game and collect some autographs. Tess already had Mia Hamm's tacked up on the bulletin board above her desk. But she had room for more.

After Tess finished her announcement, Nicole noticed her mother picking her way down the sidelines. Ms. Smith was smiling. She looked completely relaxed.

Relaxed was not her normal state. Nicole was used to seeing her doing six things at once. For years, her mother's cell phone had begun ringing during breakfast and kept ringing all day long. That morning Ms. Smith had canceled her cell phone account and shipped the slim little phone back to the company. She claimed not to miss it in the least.

"Hi, girls." Ms. Smith's voice was low and confident.

"Hi," Nicole said quietly.

Geena smiled. "Hi, Ms. Smith! How are you enjoying the game so far?"

"It's great. So fast-paced!" Ms. Smith draped an arm around Nicole's shoulders. "And, sweetie, you were right up in the action. I was proud of you."

"Mom, you obviously don't know anything about soccer," Nicole said impatiently. "Why would you be proud of me when I didn't even score?"

"Well . . . because you were trying so hard." Ms. Smith's smile had faded somewhat. "And because you were such a good sport."

The ref blew her whistle. "Players on the field!"

Nicole jumped to her feet. "Come on, Geena."

She was relieved to have an excuse to get away. Just because her mother felt a sudden need for quality time didn't mean Nicole had to provide it.

Geena smiled at Ms. Smith. "See you after the game," she said politely.

The girls walked out onto the field together. Yasmine and Tess were already standing on the halfway line. The ref was tossing the ball into the air, waiting for everyone to get into position.

Geena tapped Nicole's shoulder. "Are you mad at your mom for some reason?"

"No—for a *lot* of reasons."

Geena obviously wanted to ask more. But there wasn't time. The ref had centered the ball. She motioned for Nicole to get moving.

Nicole jogged into position. She took the kickoff quickly, passing to Tess. Tess controlled the ball, then exploded like a rocket. She two-stepped around a slow-footed Asteroid attacker. Then she continued into the center of the field, accelerating fast, the ball a blur between her feet.

A small group of the Stars' fans rose to their feet. "Go! Go! Go!"

Nicole felt a rush of pleasure as she raced up the field. She crossed to her right to fill the gap Tess had left open. This was it. They were about to score.

Tess got within ten yards of the goal before the Asteroid defenders started to threaten. Two defenders. The Asteroids were afraid of Tess. They were double-teaming her.

"Now!" Nicole shouted.

Tess shot the ball low and fast toward the goal. It hit the goalpost, bouncing toward Nicole at a difficult angle.

"Mine!" Nicole poured on the steam, her eye on the ball.

The dark-haired Asteroid was shoulder-to-shoulder with Nicole. They battled for control.

Nicole tried to focus on the ball. Her frustration was rising. Why couldn't this chick let her get off one clean shot?

The Asteroid reached out and started to draw the ball away.

"No!" Nicole yelled.

The Asteroid took control of the ball. She turned her shoulder to Nicole. Another second and she'd boot the ball out of reach.

A good sport would accept the fact that the Asteroid was a better player. Nicole thought about her mom saying *she* was a good sport. Well, now Nicole could prove that her mother didn't know anything.

Nicole pulled back and kicked the Asteroid in the knee.

THE ASTEROID FELL. SHE ROLLED OVER, HOLDING her knee.

The referee blew her whistle and waved the coach onto the field.

"Sophie!"

"Sophie, are you okay?" The Asteroids crowded around their teammate. Their coach came running. So did Mr. Thomas. His expression was grim. A couple of the girls shot angry looks at Nicole.

Nicole's face heated up. She felt as if the game had been stopped just to give everyone time to stare at her. Tess and Kyoto stood nearby. When Nicole turned toward them, they glanced away.

"Geez," Nicole muttered to herself. "It was an accident." But she knew that wasn't true. She'd kicked the Asteroid on purpose. Out of frustration. And because her mother had called her a good sport. What did her mom know, anyway?

Nicole stood staring at the Asteroids' backs. She refused to look at her mother. Was Ms. Smith embarrassed? Upset? Nicole hoped so.

A long moment passed before the Asteroid got up. She brushed off her uniform and threw Nicole a disgusted look.

"Direct free kick—Asteroids!" the ref called. "We'll resume play with a direct free kick."

Nicole couldn't resist any longer. She glanced toward the sidelines. Her mother was standing with her arms crossed, her expression stormy. Nicole felt a guilty rush of pleasure. She'd made her mother unhappy. How satisfying.

★

Tess watched the ref place the ball on the spot where Nicole had kicked the Asteroid, maybe four yards in front of the Asteroids' goal. Another Asteroid defender immediately moved into position to kick.

The Stars were standing around. They looked confused and unprepared. Nicole was staring at her cleats. Tess understood why. The Stars almost always followed the laws of the game. As a result, they didn't get much practice defending against direct kicks, which were only awarded when fouls were committed. The kick was direct, which meant the Asteroid could kick it right in for a goal. Luckily, the ball was too deep in their territory.

Tess clapped her hands loudly. "Come on, guys! Cover someone. Let's move!"

Yasmine, Nicole, and the midfielders hurriedly got into position. But by then the kicker had cleared the ball almost back to the halfway line.

As Tess watched Fiona Fagan race for the ball, her frustration rose. Nicole had broken the laws and ruined their chances of scoring.

For the rest of the game Tess tried to encourage her teammates. But the Stars weren't clicking. Geena was especially passive, letting the Asteroids run right through her. Their opponents were beating them to the ball, outplaying them, and basically making them look weak.

The Asteroids won 4 to 1. Tess was disappointed, but she knew the Stars deserved to lose. Especially Nicole.

★

Nicole's fair skin was red from running, and her blond hair was damp with sweat. She waited for Geena and gave her a nasty look.

13

"What were you doing out there?" Nicole demanded. "You practically passed the ball to the Asteroids!"

Geena stared at Nicole. She didn't understand why her friend was shouting at her. "What's the big deal?"

"In case you didn't notice, we just lost!"

"That's not *my* fault," Geena insisted. "*I* think we lost because of your foul."

"That's stupid."

"Is it?" After the foul, Geena hadn't even *wanted* to win.

"Nicole! Geena!" Ms. Smith was beckoning to them from the sidelines. "Come on, kids. I'm going to give you a ride to Regina's."

Regina's was a pizza joint down by the lake. Win or lose, Mr. Thomas and Mrs. Essex always treated the Stars to a few slices after a game.

Geena took a deep breath and tried to calm down. She knew she hadn't played her best, but she didn't want to fight with Nicole about it. "Come on, Nicole," she said. "Your mother is waiting for us."

"Let her wait." Nicole's tone was bitter.

"Are you still mad at your mother?" Geena asked.

"Mad would be an understatement."

"Why? What did she do?"

"Only ruined my life."

"How?"

"Girls!" Ms. Smith motioned for them to hurry up.

Nicole sighed again. "Come on. Let's not keep my darling mother waiting. I'll tell you what she did once we get to the restaurant."

Twenty minutes later, Nicole and Geena were seated side by side at a long table. The rest of the team was sitting at the same table, but they were keeping their distance. Geena figured they could tell that she and Nicole were having a serious conversation. Either that or they were angry about Nicole's rough play during the game.

Geena took a sip of her soda. "So what's going on with your mom?" she asked.

"She quit her job," Nicole said.

This took Geena by surprise. She'd thought Nicole was going to say that her mother was making her take piano lessons or wouldn't let her pierce her nose.

Geena took a bite of her pizza and tried to remember what Nicole had told her about her mom's job. She was a lawyer, Geena knew that much. Nicole had also told Geena that her mother worked late almost every night. She went into the office at least one day of every weekend. Geena figured that was why Ms. Smith never came to the Stars' games.

"Well, I'm sure she'll find a new one," Geena said.

Nicole shook her head. "You don't get it. She doesn't *want* a new job. She's decided to give up corporate law altogether. She's planning to open a free legal clinic."

"You mean, for homeless people and stuff like that?"

"Sort of." Nicole dropped her pizza onto her plate. "She's going to help anyone who can't afford to pay a lawyer."

Geena was impressed. "That's so radical!"

Nicole rolled her eyes. "Don't be such a flower child."

"I'm not. I just don't see what the big deal is."

"I'm worried about my mom, okay?" Nicole fiddled with her straw and looked miserable. "I mean, she's worked hard her whole entire life to get the kind of job she has now. Don't you think just giving that up is a bit weird?"

"No." Geena shrugged one shoulder. "I think it sounds like an adventure."

"I think it sounds *stupid*," Nicole said. "Yesterday she was all excited. She wanted me to see the office she rented. Geena, the place made me want to vomit. It was dirty. And it's in this grubby storefront on the south side." Nicole shuddered.

Geena shifted impatiently. The good, gooey part of her pizza was gone, so she took a bite of crust. "I'm sure it will look better once she fixes it up."

"Not as nice as her old office. It was on the fortieth floor of a skyscraper in downtown Chicago. You could see all the way to *Indiana*."

"But she wants to help poor people." Geena's tone was reasonable. "And poor people live in bad neighborhoods."

Nicole was silent.

"She's going to be helping people who really need her," Geena added.

"Yeah, well, I need her too!"

"But she's not going anywhere," Geena said. "Maybe you'll get to see her even more. I mean, she was at our game today instead of stuck in her office."

"Geena," Nicole said in a tone a parent would use with a little child. "My mom used to make *beaucoup* bucks. No more. She is going to be working for free."

"So what?" Geena said. "Your dad is a doctor. You're not in any danger of starving."

"Yeah, but my parents sold our house," Nicole said quietly. "We're moving out in twelve days."

"Bummer."

"There's more." Nicole glanced over each shoulder and motioned for Geena to come closer. "This is a total secret. If you tell anyone, I'll never speak to you again."

"What?"

Nicole dropped her voice to the barest whisper. "My dad doesn't make enough money to send three kids to private school. I have to transfer out of Country Day the week after next." Country Day was the exclusive private school Nicole attended. The place looked like a country club with blackboards.

"You're kidding me!" Geena suddenly understood why Nicole was so upset. She felt a bit ashamed that she'd given her friend such a hard time. "But you're student council president! You can't leave in the middle of the school year."

"Shhh!" Nicole shot Geena an angry look and glanced toward the end of the table.

Geena followed her gaze. Sheila was sitting in the last seat, looking beautiful as usual. Her hair was long, thick, dark, and curly. She'd pulled it into a ponytail that somehow looked glamorous.

Sheila's best friend, Rory Carver, was sitting next to her. She was listening and grinning as Sheila told some story about the game.

Geena leaned closer to Nicole and dropped her voice. "Does Sheila know you're switching schools?"

"No one does." Nicole slumped in her seat. "And it's going to be awful when she finds out."

Sheila and Nicole were fierce rivals. At the end of the previous school year, they'd both run for student council president. Sheila had done everything possible to win—including cheat. She'd been crushed when Nicole won in a landslide. Nicole had spent the past four months gloating over her victory.

Geena had helped Nicole win the election, and they'd been fast friends ever since. Geena could guess how difficult Nicole would find giving up her office. Suddenly Geena had another thought. "Wait—what school will you be going to?"

"Beachside Middle." Nicole made a disgusted face.

"Oh. Too bad you're not coming to Sacred Heart. We could be classmates."

"My parents can't afford any private school. Not even Sacred Heart."

"Oh. Well, Beachside Middle School won't be too bad. Tess and Tameka and Yaz go there. And Lacey and Fiona—"

"And Yardley and Kyoto. I know."

"Did you tell them you were switching to their school?" Geena asked.

"No! And don't you tell them either. I can't run the risk of one of them telling Sheila."

"She's going to find out eventually."

"Hopefully not until I'm out of Country Day. I don't want her to spoil my last few days there."

chapter 3

On Sunday, Tess logged on to the Internet. She surfed around until she found the number to call for tickets to the game in Chicago. She called and followed the recorded instructions until she had gathered all the information that was available. One important detail was missing. The recording didn't say when the tickets would go on sale.

Oh well, she decided. *I'll just collect the money right away. That way we'll be prepared whenever tickets are available.*

She typed the information she'd collected into the computer and printed out a copy for each of her teammates.

★

For a few minutes on Monday morning, Nicole was able to forget about all the changes in her life. She was sitting on the floor of the student council office at Country Day, counting cans of green beans, soup, and pumpkin pie filling.

"How many?" asked Rose O'Connor, a former Star.

"Two hundred and forty-three," Nicole said gleefully.

"All right," Jordan Goldman said in her quiet voice. She was another former Star—now a Galaxy player—and one of Nicole's best friends at school.

The girls exchanged high fives.

Running the Thanksgiving food drive was one of the student council's duties—and in past years the council president had *treated* it like a duty. Minimal effort. Zero enthusiasm.

Not Nicole. She'd gotten the kids interested in the food drive by setting up a competition with Geena's school, Sacred Heart. The school that collected more food would win a French fry machine that a local store had donated.

Although Thanksgiving was still two weeks away, the donations were pouring in. Even Sheila had volunteered. Nicole had given her biggest enemy the worst job: setting up a collection spot at the local supermarket.

"We're going to whump Sacred Heart," Rose said.

Nicole's smile faded. By Thanksgiving she would be attending Beachside Middle School. *She* would never get to eat French fries in the Country Day lunchroom.

★

Tess arrived at practice twenty minutes early on Tuesday afternoon. She sat on the sidelines and waited for her teammates.

Nicole got there first, climbing out of her father's white convertible. Tess proudly handed her a bright yellow information sheet. All the details on the U.S. Women's Team game were listed clearly.

Nicole scanned the paper for a few seconds, then wrinkled her nose. "What kind of printer do you have?"

"I'm not sure," Tess said. "It's a couple of years old."

"You should make your mother get a laser printer," Nicole said. "The type is much sharper."

Tess made a face. "Laser printers are awfully expensive. And this one works fine." She was happy to see Kyoto walking across the field.

Kyoto joined the other girls, and Tess gave her a copy of the information sheet. "Tickets are twenty-five dollars?" Kyoto sounded surprised. "I didn't think it would be that much."

"Me neither," Tess admitted. "But we're going to be right up front, practically in the middle of the action. Personally I'd pay twice as much to be so close to Tiffeny Milbrett." Tiffeny was another forward on the U.S. National team.

"I know what you mean," Kyoto said. "I watched a game on TV last week. Her acceleration is awesome—zero to thirty, faster than a sports car."

Kyoto and Tess were still discussing Tiffeny when Sheila and Rory arrived. Tess gave them each a paper.

"My dad can drive," Rory said. "And he wants to come to the game with us too."

"Sure," Tess said. "Just bring me enough money for two tickets." Now that their plans were starting to fall into place, Tess was getting even more excited. "You guys should try to bring me your money as soon as possible," she told them. "My mom says we need to order all the tickets at the same time. That way our seats will be together."

★

Kyoto folded the paper Tess had given her into fourths and slipped it into her pocket. The other Stars were still chatting about the game. They sounded excited. But Kyoto's enthusiasm for the trip was gone.

She doubted she'd be able to go. Kyoto didn't have twenty-five bucks. And she hated to ask her father for it.

The past few months had been rough. Back in August, when Kyoto and her father were still living in California, they'd gotten a call. Kyoto's grandmother was sick. She was in the hospital in Beachside. They should come right away.

Ever since then, Kyoto's life had been a mess. Within a few weeks her father had decided they needed to move to Beachside to care for her grandmother. They'd put their house in California on the market, packed up all their stuff, and headed out.

Kyoto knew money was tight. Her father had run his own landscaping business in California. Now he was working as a gardener. At least, when he had time to work. Lots of his energy went to taking care of his mother.

She watched and listened as Geena, Fiona, Lacey, Tameka, Yasmine, and Yardley each took a paper from Tess. Kyoto was hoping at least one of them would complain about the high price of the tickets. No one did.

Kyoto held back a sigh. It seemed as if she was the only Star who couldn't afford to go to the game.

★

"Okay, girls," Mrs. Essex said, interrupting Tess's organizing. "Plan the trip after practice. Right now it's time to warm up. Give me three laps!"

Tess, Tameka, Yasmine, and Lacey raced off. The four of them always led the team around the field. Sheila and Rory went next. The rest of the Stars fell into step behind them.

"Have you started packing yet?" Geena asked.

Nicole shrugged. "No. Stuffing things into cardboard boxes is not really my thing."

Kyoto overheard. "You're moving?"

Nicole glanced at Geena. She wasn't eager to talk about her new life. But she didn't really mind if people knew she was moving. She just wanted the fact that she was changing schools to be a secret.

Nicole shrugged. "Yeah."

"Out of Beachside?" Fiona asked breathlessly. She had asthma and allergies, which seemed to be acting up that afternoon.

"No," Nicole said. "But out of Estates on the Lake."

Estates on the Lake was the ritzy subdivision where Nicole and her family lived. Their house had six bedrooms and an enormous lawn. Nicole loved the spacious house and her big pink room on the second floor.

That morning her mother had dumped a stack of cardboard boxes at the foot of Nicole's bed. Nicole was supposed to start packing that evening. And lots of her stuff had to go to charity. Her new bedroom was only about half the size of her old one.

"At least you're not moving far," Kyoto said. "Like to another time zone. And to a place with weird seasons like winter."

Nicole knew that before Kyoto had moved to Michigan from California, she'd never even *seen* snow.

"I, for one, am glad that you had to move so far," Yardley told Kyoto.

"Me too," Geena added. "And I promise to make you love winter. We'll go sledding and ice-skating—and we'll teach you how to play indoor soccer."

Kyoto grinned. "Thanks, guys."

Nicole waited impatiently for her friends' attention. "I'm glad we're not leaving Beachside," she said. "But wait until you guys see our new house— that is, *if* I let you come over. The place is an embarrassment."

The girls reached the end of the field. They turned the corner, marched around the goalposts, and kept going.

The other girls didn't say anything. Nicole could tell they didn't really feel sorry for her yet.

"The place is a shack," she said firmly. "And the neighborhood is dangerous."

"Dangerous?" Now Geena looked worried.

Nicole bit her lip. Dangerous was an exaggeration. But she couldn't admit that now. She decided to change the subject.

"Guess what the name of the street is?" Nicole said.

Geena shrugged.

"What?" Fiona asked.

"Gray Lane!" Nicole announced. "Isn't that the worst street name in the world?"

"Well, it is kind of depressing," Yard admitted.

Nicole nodded. "And I'm depressed too, just thinking about moving."

chapter 4

"HEY, YARD, WAIT UP!" FIONA CALLED AF-
ter practice.

Yard turned around and gave Fiona a lopsided
grin. Her bangs were sticking straight out, and
her T-shirt was tucked into only one side of her
sweatpants.

Fiona bit back a smile. Something about Yard's
thrown-together look was endearing.

"Heading home?" Yard asked. The girls had just
discovered that they lived a few blocks apart. Both
of their houses were in the historic center of town,
a section full of wooden houses with big porches.

"Yup." Fiona groaned. "I have about three
hours of homework tonight. Research paper for
history."

"What's the topic?"

"Decisive battles of the Civil War."

"Ew—brutal."

The girls turned right on North Lake Street, Beachside's main drag. Yard was telling Fiona about a cool online encyclopedia as they turned down Beach Street. But she stopped dead at the first corner they got to.

"Look!" She pointed up at the street sign.

Fiona looked up. "Gray Lane. Hey, isn't that Nicole's new street?"

Yardley looked confused. "She did say she was moving to Gray Lane. But she couldn't have meant *this* Gray Lane."

Fiona turned around. Shoppers were strolling down North Lake, maybe fifty yards away. A group of tourists was posing for a picture in front of a beautiful old house with a big sugar maple. This was one of Beachside's oldest and nicest neighborhoods.

"Come on." Yardley took Fiona's hand. "I've got to know for sure."

Fiona and Yardley walked down Gray Lane together. The street was narrower than Beach. Beautiful old shade trees towered over their heads. The six houses that lined the street weren't big, but each one was in perfect condition. The paint was fresh, the yards were filled with flowers, and expensive cars were parked in the driveways.

"Check out that white convertible," Yardley said.

Fiona recognized the car immediately. The car was Dr. Philips's pride. It was an old Mustang, white with a red interior. The car was parked in front of the largest and most elaborate house on the lane. A fountain bubbled in front of the door, and Fiona could see a greenhouse in the side yard.

"Some shack," Fiona said.

Yardley shook her head impatiently. "Nicole Philips-Smith is the biggest whiner I've ever met!"

★

"Dad! Where are you?" Nicole shouted as she walked into her house just before dinner. She and Geena had gone shopping after practice. Nicole had spent the last of her allowance on a new sweater, and she was flat broke. Not that she was worried. Nicole's dad was always happy to hand over some extra cash—which was exactly what she needed for the trip to Chicago.

Nicole walked through the kitchen, the dining room, the living room, the family room, the laundry room, and the playroom. No Dad. The door of the first-floor powder room was open. The little room was empty.

"Dad!" Nicole and Geena started up the back stairway.

"I'm up here!"

Dr. Philips's voice was coming from the attic, a space Nicole's family rarely used. *What is he doing up there?* Nicole wondered, starting up the narrow flight of uncarpeted steps.

"What are you doing?" Nicole asked as she reached the top of the steps.

"Packing."

Nicole frowned when she realized that both her parents were in the attic. They were surrounded by stuff Nicole hadn't seen in years. Old dolls she'd outgrown. Five pairs of dusty skis and ski boots. Boxes marked BOYS' BABY CLOTHES. A marble coffee table the family had used for about a month before Ms. Smith had decided it was ugly. An old guitar that belonged to Nicole's brother Tyler.

"What are you going to do with all this junk?"

Nicole's mother sighed. Her nose was smudged with dust, and her hair was coming out of her ponytail. She looked tired. "Give it away, I guess."

"No!" Nicole said. "Some of this stuff is mine! You can't give it away without even asking me!"

Ms. Smith looked doubtful. "Nicole, you haven't used any of this stuff in years."

"So what?" Nicole grabbed a doll in a pink-and-white-striped dress and hugged her close. Her name was Lulu Belle. Nicole's grandmother had given her that doll on her fifth birthday. "You were going to give my old dolls away?"

"Why not?"

"Because they're *mine*," Nicole said.

"They're just gathering dust up here," Ms. Smith argued.

Nicole's dad cleared his throat. "Nicole, you can keep your dolls if you like. Just remember that everything you pack needs to fit into the new house."

"I don't see why we have to move in the first place," Nicole grumbled.

Nicole's father looked sympathetic. But her mother sighed impatiently. "Nicole, we've been over and over that," she said. "Let's talk about something else. How was practice today?"

"Fine," Nicole said sullenly. "We're all going to see the Women's National Team play in Chicago."

She reached for another doll—her first Barbie. She couldn't believe her mother would give these away.

"That sounds like fun," Dr. Philips said.

"I need twenty-five dollars for the ticket," Nicole said.

Dr. Philips started to reach for his wallet. But Ms. Smith held out a hand, stopping him. "Nicole, what happened to your allowance?"

"I spent it."

Ms. Smith frowned. "Listen, kiddo, we're all trying to tighten our belts a little around here. Why don't you pay for the ticket out of your next allowance?"

"Fine, but I need the money now. May I have an advance on my next allowance?"

"No."

"No?" Nicole wailed. "Why not?"

"Because I think it would be better if you learned the value of money," Ms. Smith said. "You can earn the twenty-five dollars."

"Doing what?"

"Packing up the kitchen dishes," Ms. Smith said.

"No way! That will take forever." Besides, Nicole didn't want to do anything to help with the move.

"Then you'd better get started."

Nicole looked at her father for help, but he just shrugged. She turned around and stomped downstairs. She went to her room, lay down on her bed, and balanced Barbie and Lulu Belle on her stomach. If her parents wouldn't give her the money for the game, fine. She'd get the money some other way.

★

That evening Yasmine's stomach was rumbling as she slipped into a booth at the new Chinese restaurant on North Lake Street. Her family was eating dinner late because Mr. and Mrs. Madrigal had gone to a parents' meeting at Beachside Middle School.

Yago, Yasmine's twin brother, sat next to her. He immediately slouched down in the seat and started reading a comic book.

"Yasmine, guess who we met at your school?" Mrs. Madrigal said, beaming.

"Who?"

Mr. Madrigal held up both hands. "Order first. Chat second. I'm starving."

"Okay." Mrs. Madrigal opened her menu. "I think I'll get chicken with cashew nuts."

Mr. Madrigal nodded. "Mmm. That sounds good."

Yasmine didn't even bother to open her menu. "Szechuan beef. So who did you meet?"

"Szechuan beef?" Mrs. Madrigal asked. "Are you sure? That's so spicy."

"That's why I like it."

"Sounds good to me," Mr. Madrigal said.

Yago picked up his straw and shot the wrapper toward the ceiling. "I'm getting the sweet-and-sour shrimp."

"Mmm," Mr. Madrigal said. "Great choice."

"Daddy!" Yasmine made a face.

"What?"

"You're practically drooling on the table!"

"Sorry." Mr. Madrigal laughed. "I'm just hungry."

The waiter approached. He put down a pot of tea and took the Madrigals' order. Yasmine's father ordered hot-and-sour soup, cold sesame noodles, and honey spareribs.

Yasmine picked up the teapot. She poured a tiny cup for each member of her family. "So who did you guys meet?"

Yago peeked over his comic book.

"Ms. Smith!" Yasmine's mother looked pleased.

"Nicole's mom?"

"Yes."

Yago made a disappointed face and went back to reading. He was interested in only two of Yasmine's teammates—Lacey and Sheila. He probably liked them because they were always flirting with him. Yasmine couldn't believe her friends actually thought Yago was cute.

"She's such a sweet lady!" Mrs. Madrigal continued. "I'm sorry we never met before."

"Did she tell you she quit her high-powered job to open a free legal clinic on the south side?" Mr. Madrigal asked.

Mrs. Madrigal nodded. "It's about time someone did."

"That's nice," Yasmine said. "But I don't understand. What was Nicole's mother doing at Beachside Middle School?"

"Didn't you know?" Mrs. Madrigal looked surprised. "Nicole is transferring."

"She is?"

Mrs. Madrigal nodded, looking absolutely sure. "Next week, her mom said."

"*That's* interesting," Yasmine said. She thought it was very mysterious that Nicole hadn't told her herself. Oh, well. Maybe she'd just forgotten. The important thing was that Yasmine had found out in time to welcome her in style.

★

"Nicole is transferring to Beachside Middle School!" Yasmine announced the next morning. She was walking to school with Tess and Tameka, and they were running late.

"Are you sure?" Tess asked.

"Sure I'm sure."

"Why didn't she tell us?" Tameka stopped and put down her books. She needed both hands to struggle with the zipper on her windbreaker. The wind was really whipping.

"I don't know," Yasmine admitted. "But her mom told my mom. She's starting a week from today."

"Hurry up," Tess urged Tameka. "We've got five minutes until the bell."

"All right, all right." Tameka finally got the zipper to work. She grabbed her books, and the girls started to walk fast.

Tess was a few steps ahead. "It's weird imagining Nicole at our school," she said. "She's totally not going to fit in."

Yasmine nodded, imagining the matching designer outfits Nicole wore. She was always color coordinated. She wore her hair smoothed back by a headband. She had a collection of anklets with lace on them.

39

Lace and headbands and designer clothes were not big at Beachside Middle School. Most of Yasmine's classmates dressed in gym shoes, jeans, and sweatshirts.

"She's going to be like a foreigner," Tameka said.

The girls were still racing down the sidewalk. Another two blocks and they'd be able to see the school building.

"Confused by the local customs," Tess said with a giggle. "Unable to communicate with the natives!"

Yasmine thought Tess was spending too much time with Yardley. She was starting to develop a strange sense of humor. "Maybe we should give Nicole a guidebook," she said.

Tess turned back and smiled. "That's a great idea. We'll write her a guide to surviving Beachside Middle School. We can give it to her as a present on her first day."

"No, before that," Tameka said. "We want to give her time to study."

The bell rang. They still had a block to go.

"Agreed!" Tess said as she started to run. "Let's work on it tonight!"

chapter 5

By nine o'clock that evening, Nicole's guidebook had grown to seven pages and covered everything from teachers to cute boys.

"We should warn her about the noodle casserole," Tameka said. She was lying on Tess's bed, staring thoughtfully up at the ceiling. Textbooks, notebooks, pencils, calculators, and snacks littered the room.

Tess was seated at the computer. "I actually took a bite of that stuff once. I can still remember the texture of it. It was"—she shuddered—"slimy."

"Ew!" Yasmine exclaimed. "Put it in. But personally, I think you'd have to be crazy to order that stuff. I mean, it's *purple*. How good could it taste?"

Tess reached back and gave Yasmine a playful shove. "Who are you calling crazy?"

"Eggplant is purple," Tameka said. "And plums. And grapes. Purple isn't the problem. Noodle casserole is the problem."

"Nicole is going to love this," Tess said, typing rapidly.

"She won't know how to thank us," Tameka predicted.

★

Tameka, Tess, and Yasmine rode to Thursday's practice with Mr. Thomas. He ran into another coach in the parking lot and stopped to chat.

The girls walked over to the field. Yasmine was carrying the guidebook. She'd wrapped it in pink tissue paper and put on a gold bow.

Tameka lay down on the grass. The sun felt terrific on her face, and she closed her eyes. "Ahhh," she sighed.

Tess nudged Tameka's leg with her cleat. "Come on. Let's juggle or do something to warm up."

"Can't," Tameka told her. "I'm watching for Nicole."

"Your eyes are closed."

"That's what makes it so challenging."

Tess made an impatient noise, which made Tameka smile. The girl just didn't know how to relax.

Yasmine put Nicole's present down on Tameka's belly. "I'm in!"

Tess smiled and dropped her soccer ball between her feet. "Come and get it," she said.

Yasmine ran toward Tess. But Tess shot off across the field, dribbling skillfully. "Whoops! You missed!"

Tameka enjoyed the sunshine for almost ten minutes before she heard Nicole's voice and sat up. Nicole was walking across the field with Geena. Tess and Yasmine had seen them too. They came running.

"Ta-da!" Tameka held the package out to Nicole.

Nicole's face lit up. "What is this?"

"Open it and find out," Tess said. "It's from all three of us."

Nicole tore open the tissue paper and pulled out the little booklet they had made. " 'The Unofficial Guide to Surviving Beachside Middle School,' " she read from the cover. Her expression darkened and she gave Geena an angry look. "How did you guys know I'm transferring?"

"Don't look at me!" Geena exclaimed. "I didn't tell them."

"My mom saw your mom at the parents' meeting Tuesday night," Yasmine explained.

"Oh."

"Are you going to read the guide?" Yasmine asked. "We put a bunch of top-secret information in there. We even got Lacey to give us a list of the five cutest boys in school."

"You told Lacey?" Nicole's eyes were wide with horror.

"Sure," Tess said. "What's the big deal?"

"The big deal is that I don't want Sheila to know I'm leaving Country Day," Nicole said. "You guys have to keep this a secret."

Tameka shot Tess an uncertain look. She knew that Nicole and Sheila didn't get along. But Nicole was totally overreacting.

Tess shrugged. "Okay. We won't tell."

Tameka nodded.

"Whatever," Yasmine said.

Nicole seemed to relax a tiny bit. "Thanks, you guys. Just keep this a secret until Wednesday. That's my first day at Beachside Middle School."

"Okay," Yasmine said. "Do you know what room you're going to be in?"

"I hope you're in our class," Tameka added. "Our teacher, Mrs. Keene, is a sweetheart."

Nicole laughed. "Thanks. But I don't think it's likely that we'll be in class together."

"Why not?" Tameka asked.

"Well." Nicole smiled smugly. "I'm sure I'll be attending the Gifted and Talented class."

Tameka frowned. The Gifted and Talented class was *not* her favorite topic of discussion. She had never understood why the teachers thought Tess and Yardley were smart enough to be in the special class but she and Yasmine and Kyoto weren't. Tameka had decided to prove she was gifted and talented too, and had been working extra hard at school that year.

"What do you mean you're sure?" Tameka couldn't help sounding annoyed. "Did the school say you were going to be in Hollinsworth's class or not?"

"They didn't *tell* me that," Nicole said casually. "I just know. After all, I've had years of superior private education. Hollinsworth's class is going to be a breeze for me."

Tameka shot Yasmine a frustrated look. She

was starting to feel insulted. Nicole seemed to be saying that attending her snotty private school made her smarter than public-school kids.

Yardley ran up to the group. "Hey, Tess, I've got my ticket money." She handed Tess a twenty and a five.

"Thanks," Tess said.

Tameka waited until Nicole ran over to the other side of the field to talk to Lacey and Fiona. Then she told Yasmine, "I hope she does end up in Hollinsworth's class."

Tess overheard. "Hey, no way. I hope *you* get her."

★

Before practice began, Tess collected money from Fiona, Sheila, and Rory. "I've got a hundred bucks in my pocket," she told Tameka. "I feel a little funny running around with that much money."

Tameka made a face. "I don't think you should keep it in your pocket during practice. Listen, why don't you get Dad's car keys? You can put your backpack in his trunk until after practice."

"Sounds like a plan," Tess said. She got the keys and trotted over to the car. She was on her way back to the field when she saw Kyoto walking across the parking lot toward her.

"Can I talk to you for a minute?" Kyoto looked terrific as usual. She was dressed for practice in baggy black shorts and a skinny red T-shirt. She had wrapped silver duct tape around her cleats for some reason, and that looked fantastic too.

"Sure." Tess felt a bit dumpy in her Disneyland T-shirt and blue biking shorts. "What's up?" she asked as she headed back toward the field.

Kyoto put out a hand to stop her. "I was hoping we could talk alone. . . ."

"Oh—no problem." Practice wouldn't start for a few minutes. Tess leaned against a car bumper.

"It's about the trip to Chicago." Kyoto crossed her arms and looked down at the ground. "I can't go."

Tess felt a stab of disappointment. "Why not?" she wailed. "It's almost two weeks away. You have plenty of time to change any plans you've already made."

"That's not it." Kyoto looked up and met Tess's gaze. She shrugged. "My dad won't cough up the cash for the ticket."

"Oh." Tess was bummed out. She wanted all the

Stars to go to the game. She knew they'd have a great time. And she wanted her teammates to watch her heroes in action—to see how well women could play soccer.

Tess thought about the thirty dollars she had in her top desk drawer. She'd earned ten helping the Thomases clean out their garage. Her grandmother had sent Tess the other twenty dollars when she'd earned an A on a tough math test. Tess had been planning to put the money into her college fund. But college was six years away, and besides, Tess was planning on getting a soccer scholarship.

Kyoto gave Tess a nudge. "Come on. Mrs. Essex is probably waiting for us."

Tess didn't move. "Why don't I lend you the money?" she offered.

"No thanks," Kyoto said.

"Why not?"

"Um . . ." Kyoto shifted her weight uneasily. "I don't know when I could pay you back."

"Whenever you get your allowance."

Kyoto smiled. "That's just the thing. I don't get an allowance."

No allowance? Tess thought. *How does Kyoto survive?* "I don't mind waiting," she said.

"I wouldn't feel right about that," Kyoto answered.

"Maybe you could earn it baby-sitting," Tess said.

Kyoto shook her head. "My dad thinks I'm too young to baby-sit. He doesn't like the idea of my coming home after dark."

Tess was still trying to think of a solution. But Kyoto seemed to be losing patience with their conversation. "Come on, I don't want to miss warm-up."

The girls started toward the field together. They were passing the rest rooms when Tess stopped.

"I've got it!" she exclaimed. "How about if the whole team helped you raise the money? We could have an event. Like Farm Aid. Only ours will be Kyoto Aid!"

Kyoto looked horrified. She shook her head rapidly, her eyes wide. "Please don't do that," she begged. "That would make me feel totally strange."

"But—" Tess started to argue.

"Listen," Kyoto pleaded. "I don't mind missing the game that much. And you can tell me all about it when you get home."

"Well . . . okay," Tess said slowly. She wasn't ready to give up.

"Promise?" Kyoto still sounded worried.

"Cross my heart," Tess said. "I'll forget about it."

But Tess *couldn't* forget about it. She knew Kyoto was disappointed about missing the game. And she was disappointed too.

The team did their warm-up laps. Mrs. Essex led them in a toe-to-neck stretch. Tess relaxed as they moved through the familiar routine. She always loved to exercise. But working out with the team was especially nice.

She looked around the circle at all the familiar faces. Tess had fought and laughed with most of her teammates. A few knew her deepest, darkest secrets. Some were her best friends.

Even more importantly, they were a team. And teams worked together to win games—and to solve problems. Tess knew the Stars would want to help Kyoto get a ticket to the game in Chicago.

She considered telling them Kyoto didn't have the money to buy one. But she sensed that was the wrong thing to do. Kyoto had seemed . . . not embarrassed, exactly, but uneasy about her situation. Obviously her family couldn't afford the ticket right now.

"Okay, girls," Mr. Thomas said. "Let's work on ball control. Choose a partner and grab a ball."

Tameka motioned to Tess, and they stood together.

"Take turns throwing the ball to your partner," Mr. Thomas instructed them. "Aim high sometimes, low sometimes. When you're receiving the ball, I want to see you control it on the first touch of your foot and prepare for the next move on the second touch. Mrs. Essex and I will walk around and see how you're doing."

Tameka tossed Tess the ball. "I'll receive first," she said.

"Okay."

The girls positioned themselves about three feet apart. The drill was simple. It was good practice for beginning players like Yardley but a bit elementary for Tameka. Tess decided to make the drill as difficult as possible. She tossed the ball way up in the air. Even Tameka wasn't very good at heading balls.

"Thanks a lot!" Tameka shouted as she positioned herself under the ball. It hit her on top of her head and bounced behind her. Tameka groaned and ran after it.

Tess looked across the field. Lacey was messing

around, throwing the ball to Fiona before she was ready to receive it. Geena was working with Nicole. Sheila and Rory were over in front of one goal.

Tess had an awful thought as she watched the Stars. What if other members of the team couldn't afford a ticket to the National Team game either? Tess had practically *demanded* that her teammates bring their money in as soon as possible.

Who still hadn't brought it?

Nicole—but she'd probably just forgotten. Everyone knew that Nicole's family had plenty of money. Her mom was a lawyer. Her dad was a doctor. End of story.

Tameka—but Tess was practically a member of the Thomases' family, and she knew they weren't having any financial problems. The same was true for Yasmine.

But what about Geena? She'd told Tess she'd bring the money to the game on Saturday. But could she afford it? Geena had six little brothers and sisters. And her mother was a full-time mom.

And Lacey! Her mother worked as an aerobics instructor. She couldn't make much money. Neither could Lacey's father, who was a cop. Tess had never really thought about it before, but Lacey's family lived in a little house with hardly any yard.

Tess began to wish she hadn't run around ordering her teammates to pay for this game. Even the girls who had already brought in their money might be wishing they could have gotten out of it. Tess knew she had to do something to fix her big mistake.

chapter 6

TESS WAITED UNTIL PRACTICE ENDED. THEN she pulled Kyoto aside. "I have an idea," she whispered.

"Tess, let's drop—"

"Just listen," Tess insisted. "What if the team raised enough money to pay for all our tickets? That way you won't have to feel singled out."

Tess bit her lip and gave Kyoto a minute to think it over. She crossed her fingers for good luck. Kyoto was quiet for a long moment. Her expression was difficult to read.

"Do you really want me to go that badly?" Kyoto finally asked.

"Of course!"

Kyoto broke into a huge smile. "That's great, because I really, really want to go!"

Tess glanced around the field. The Stars had started to wander off. Tess put two fingers between her lips and let out a piercing whistle. Everyone turned to stare at her.

"I need to talk to all the Stars!" Tess shouted. "Meet me by Mr. Thomas's car!"

Most of the girls looked curious. Nicole's expression was slightly annoyed. But everyone changed direction and began walking toward the car.

Kyoto shook her head. "You don't waste any time, do you?"

Tess just shrugged happily. She was pleased that Kyoto had agreed with her plan.

Mr. Thomas was standing by the equipment locker, showing Saturday's lineup to Mrs. Essex. Tess ran over to him. "May I borrow your car keys again?" she asked. "I have to get my backpack."

Mr. Thomas pulled the keys out of his pocket and handed them to Tess. Tess ran over to the car, where the team had already gathered. She unlocked the trunk, took out her backpack, and pulled out the ticket money.

"I'm going to give money back to those of you

who have already paid me for the game in Chicago," she announced.

"What's going on?" Fiona asked.

"Aren't we going to the game?" Tameka asked.

"Yes!" Tess said. "But I have a great idea! I think we should raise the money for our tickets."

"Why?" Nicole looked annoyed.

"Because . . ." Tess thought fast. She couldn't tell the team the real reason. But they weren't going to agree to do a lot of hard work without some sort of explanation. Like . . . Tess's brain stalled.

"I think we'll enjoy the game more if we *earn* the right to attend," Kyoto added helpfully.

Fiona was smiling. "I agree."

"Me too," Geena said. "Besides, I need that money for a new snowboarding jacket."

Nicole shot Geena an impatient look. "Well, I hate this idea. What are we going to do, have a lemonade stand?"

"Maybe," Tess said hotly. "What's wrong with a lemonade stand?"

"Nothing, if you're six years old," Nicole said. "I don't know about the rest of you, but I have better ways to spend my time."

"Yeah, like sharpening your fangs," Sheila muttered.

Rory laughed. Everyone else pretended not to hear her.

Nicole stood up straighter. "What is the big deal? It will be much easier if everyone just pays their own way."

"Easier for you, maybe!" Tess shot back. "But—" She bit her lip, narrowly avoiding spitting out Kyoto's secret.

"But what?"

"Nothing," Tess muttered.

Yardley glanced at Tess. She'd been listening carefully, and she seemed to guess at some of the motivation behind the sudden change in plans.

"Nicole," Yardley said in a quiet voice that was hard to ignore. "What if some of us don't have the money for a ticket?"

"Whoever can pay should go," Nicole replied immediately. "Everyone else can watch the game on ESPN."

Geena poked Nicole with her elbow. "Come on. Raising the money together will be fun."

"No thanks," Nicole said. "I have my entire

room to pack. That's about as much fun as I can handle."

"Well, I'm in," Sheila said. She'd support anything Nicole was against.

"Me too," Rory said.

Fiona and Lacey exchanged looks.

Yardley glanced at her watch.

"Well," Tess said, "why don't we vote on it? Everyone who wants to raise the money for our tickets, raise your hand."

Sheila's and Rory's hands shot up. Kyoto and Yardley raised theirs. So did Tameka and Yasmine and Tess. Fiona and Lacey were a little hesitant, but they too showed they were in. Geena gave Nicole a pleading look and raised her hand.

Nicole stood with her hands on her hips. "Just because you guys want to do this doesn't mean *I* have to help."

Tess couldn't believe how difficult Nicole was being. "If you don't want to help, that's fine. The rest of us can raise the money without you."

Nicole felt uneasy as she waited for her father to pick her up from practice. She couldn't help feeling suspicious about Tess's sudden desire to raise money for the game.

Did Geena tell Tess Mom quit her job? Nicole wondered.

The thought was ridiculous. Geena would never betray her trust. Still, Nicole just couldn't get the idea out of her mind. The last thing she needed was to have the Stars treating her as if she didn't have enough money for a stupid ticket to a soccer game.

All the Stars knew Nicole had money. They expected her to throw parties and buy them nice birthday presents. Nicole couldn't guess how they'd act if they suddenly thought she was poor. Maybe they'd dump her. Maybe they'd start liking Sheila instead. *She* had plenty of money.

Dr. Philips's car pulled into view. Nicole decided that she had to keep up appearances with her teammates. And that meant she wasn't getting anywhere near Tess's stupid lemonade stand. She'd get the money some other way. And if she couldn't, she'd just stay home.

★

Saturday's weather—overcast with a sharp bite in the air—made Tess think of pumpkins and apple cider. The leaves on the trees beside the playing field had turned red and yellow.

Tess shivered as she climbed out of Mr.

Thomas's car. She wished she had worn sweats under her team shorts.

Fiona was already waiting on the field, and she immediately approached Tess, Tameka, and Yasmine. "Guess what?" Fiona said. "Tickets to the Women's National soccer game go on sale Thursday!"

"How do you know?" Tess asked.

"My dad is working on a story." Fiona's father was an editor at *The Beachside Times*. "The reporter said the tickets are expected to sell out within hours."

"That's bad," Tameka said. "We need a bunch of tickets all together."

Fiona nodded. "I think Tess's mom should call in the order on Thursday morning."

Yasmine shook her head. "One problem. That doesn't give us much time to raise the money."

"We haven't even decided what to do yet," Tameka pointed out.

"We've got four days," Fiona said.

Yasmine shook her head. "That's not enough time."

"Whoa!" Tess called. "Everyone calm down. Four days is plenty of time. We just need to start planning."

By the time the game started, all the Stars knew they had just been handed a deadline. But for the next hour they didn't have time to think about anything but soccer.

The Meteors scored less than a minute into the game.

"That's okay!" Tess clapped her hands loudly. "Let's tie it up!"

Fiona, Yasmine, and Geena were playing on the front line. Tess, who was playing right midfielder, kept feeding them the ball. They tried to score a dozen times in the first half. But the Meteors kept pushing them back.

At halftime, the score remained Meteors 1, Stars 0.

"You guys are playing great!" Mr. Thomas told the team. "You're totally dominating the game. Just keep shooting until one goes in."

Tess was fired up as she jogged onto the field. Ten minutes into the second half, Fiona got close enough to shoot. Her kick was powerful. The ball sped through the grass. But the Meteor goalkeeper dived for it and caught it.

"Come on, you guys!" Tess hollered. "We can do this!"

Players on both teams looked worn out. Now was

the time to punch through the Meteors' defense. If only Tess could keep her teammates fighting to get the ball in the goal.

Five minutes later Yasmine got the ball. She drove it down the left side of the field and sent it into the middle. Fiona intercepted the bouncing ball and ripped a right-footed volley into the left side of the net. The Meteors' goalkeeper couldn't get there in time.

"Goal—Stars!" the ref called.

"Yes!" Mr. Thomas shouted from the sidelines.

The Stars' fans were on their feet, cheering.

Tess ran over to Yasmine and gave her a big hug. So did everyone else on the team. "Just one more!" Tess said as the team broke up.

The chance didn't come until almost six minutes later. Tess picked up a pass from Rory and began to drive for the goal. Ignoring how heavy her legs felt, she two-stepped around a Meteor midfielder and kept going.

A burly Meteor defender charged. Tess picked up the pace and left her in the dust. From ten yards out, she shot. The ball hit the crossbar and bounced in behind the goalkeeper.

"Goal—Stars!" the ref called.

"All right!" Tameka shouted.

Tess found herself surrounded by her teammates. Everyone was laughing and shouting and congratulating her. She couldn't stop grinning. What a rush!

Finally the ref called an end to the celebration. The last two minutes of the game were uneventful. Final score: Stars 2, Meteors 1.

Tess was on top of the world. If the Stars could win this game, they could do anything.

chapter 7

An hour later the Stars were gathered around a table at Regina's. They were still reliving their victory when Tess rose to her feet.

"Hey, you guys!" she called.

Except for Tameka and Yasmine, nobody paid any attention. The restaurant was full and noisy. Besides the Stars, several other AYSO teams were eating. The jukebox was playing, and the cashier was shouting out the numbers of the orders that were ready to be picked up.

Tess climbed up on her chair. "You guys!"

Now she had their attention.

Tess smiled at her teammates. "We've got to decide how we're going to raise the money for

Chicago," she said. "And we've got to do it before we go home this afternoon. It has to be something simple that doesn't take a lot of preparation."

The girls munched in silence for a few minutes. Tess climbed off her chair, sat down, and sipped her soda thoughtfully.

Tameka was the first to speak. "Um . . . we could walk dogs," she offered tentatively.

"I'm allergic," Fiona said immediately.

"We could rake leaves," Geena said.

"I'm allergic," Fiona said with a slight smile.

"How about a bake sale?" Lacey asked.

"We'd have to spend a lot of money on ingredients," Yasmine pointed out.

"We could just pay our own ways," Nicole said.

Several girls shot her impatient looks, and she slumped down in her seat.

Tess groaned in frustration. They were wasting time. They needed an idea—a good idea—now. She tried to force herself to concentrate, but nothing came to her.

She saw Sheila get up and walk over to the jukebox. *Great. We'll never figure this out if people start wandering away.* Tess's gaze fell on Yardley, who was sitting at the end of the table. She was reading a book about Mozart and seemed quite engrossed.

"Yardley, would you please pay attention?" Tess asked in a grumpy voice.

Yard looked up as if startled. She reluctantly closed her book and smiled at Tess. "What are we talking about?"

"How to raise money for Chicago!"

"Why don't we have a car wash?" Yardley said.

Tess looked at Tameka and Yasmine.

"We wouldn't need any major supplies," Yasmine said.

"No, it would be a very inexpensive fundraiser," Yardley said. "The only downside is that it's weather-dependent. A cold snap or a rainy day would put us out of business. But I checked the long-range forecast, and things look good for the next five days."

"Hey, Dad!" Tameka called. Mr. Thomas, Mrs. Essex, and a couple of other parents were at the next table. "Can we have a car wash in our driveway? It's to raise money for the trip to Chicago."

Mr. Thomas gave the girls a wink. "Sure. Ask nicely and I'll even let you use the hose."

"Thanks!" Tameka said.

Yasmine snapped her fingers. "My mom has a

special car vacuum with all these attachments. I'm sure she'd let us borrow it."

Just like that, Tess felt the tension lift. Everyone was grinning and nodding.

"We should hang a couple of big signs at busy intersections," Yardley said.

Tess started taking notes on her napkin. "Let's make the posters tomorrow at my house," she suggested.

The girls spent the next ten minutes dividing up tasks. Pulling off the car wash was going to take some organization. But Tess could feel that it would work.

★

Sheila walked over to the jukebox and pulled a dollar out of her pocket. Yago Madrigal was already standing next to the glowing machine, studying the selections. He looked as adorable as ever. His yellow uniform looked great with his dark hair.

"Hey."

"Hey." Yago gave her a shy smile.

Sheila fed her money into the machine. "I get four selections," she told Yago. "How about if I make two and you make two?"

"Sure."

For a moment the two were quiet as they studied their choices. Then Yago quickly punched in some numbers, turned around, and leaned against the machine. "Looks like you guys are celebrating," he said.

"We won."

"Oh. I thought maybe it was because of Nicole."

Sheila was still studying the list of songs. A moment passed before she realized she didn't have any idea what Yago was talking about.

"What about Nicole?" she asked warily. The way Yago was talking, it sounded as if Nicole had won a prize or something. *Please don't let it be that*, Sheila thought. The girl was already a pain. She didn't need an even bigger head.

"She's transferring to Beachside Middle School," Yago said casually.

For a moment Sheila thought Yago must be lying. Nicole transferring? That would just be too good to be believed. Like winning the lottery without buying a ticket, or falling asleep in French class and waking up in France.

Sheila felt like spinning in circles, like singing, like kissing Yago's handsome face. This was just great!

She said goodbye to Yago as quickly as possible, rushed back to the Stars' table, and whispered the news in Rory's ear.

Rory looked skeptical. "But why would she transfer?"

Sheila knew there was one big reason kids transferred from superexpensive Country Day to public school—which was free. "I bet her parents can't afford the tuition anymore."

Yasmine was sitting on Rory's other side. "What are you guys whispering about? It looks juicy."

Sheila answered carefully. "I just heard that Nicole's father got fired. I don't know whether to believe it."

Yasmine shook her head rapidly. "Her dad didn't get fired! Her mom quit her job."

Sheila fought back a smile. This was even better than she had imagined. Not only was Nicole transferring, she was transferring because she was poor. Nicole would be totally humiliated if anyone at Country Day found out.

Sheila waited until Yasmine went off to get another slice of pizza, then motioned for Rory to come closer. "Let's give Nicole a little going-away present," she whispered.

★

On Sunday afternoon Tameka, Yasmine, Kyoto, and Yardley all gathered in Tess's kitchen. Tess dumped some poster board and markers on the table.

"I made a sample poster last night," Yasmine said. "What do you guys think?" She proudly held up her sign. It read:

Get your car washed by Stars!

Help kids see the greatest soccer players alive!

Only $

"I'll put in a big arrow after that first line so they know where to turn," Yasmine said. "But I don't know how much we should charge."

"The big car wash on Reading Road charges five dollars," Kyoto said. She was leaning against the sink.

Tameka was sitting cross-legged on the floor in front of the refrigerator. She made a face. "Yeah, but you have to do all the work yourself at that place. Basically, they're renting you a hose. It's a total ripoff."

"So . . . maybe we should charge six bucks." Yasmine twirled the marker and looked thoughtful.

Yardley quickly shook her head. "That's not enough. At twenty-five dollars apiece, ten tickets will cost us two hundred and fifty dollars. If we charge six dollars per car, we'll have to wash forty-one and two-thirds cars to earn enough money. I doubt we'll have that much business."

Tess smiled happily. She loved it when Yardley spouted numbers. It was a lot like watching Briana Scurry stop a blistering shot. A display of remarkable talent.

Yasmine was staring. "Do you do that in your head?"

Yardley nodded. "Can't you?"

"Oh, sure," Yasmine said weakly.

"One question," Tess told Yardley. "Why only ten tickets? There are eleven Stars."

"But Nicole is refusing to help," Yardley pointed out. "*We're* not going to earn money for *her* ticket, are we?"

"No way!" Yasmine said.

"I don't think so," Tameka added.

Tess shrugged. She wanted all the Stars at the game. But she didn't have any problem with Nicole's paying for her own ticket.

"So what should we charge?" Yasmine asked.

The kitchen got quiet. Everyone looked at Yardley.

"Ten dollars," Yard said firmly. "Making change will be easy. And we'll only need to wash twenty-five cars."

"Do you really think people will pay that much?" Kyoto asked.

Yardley nodded. "They're not just getting a car wash, they're helping a bunch of kids."

★

On Monday afternoon Jordan walked with Nicole toward her locker. Nicole was thinking that she had only one more day at Country Day. She was relieved that none of the Stars had told Sheila her big secret.

"What's that in front of your locker?" Jordan asked.

Nicole squinted. "It looks like a fruit basket."

The girls got closer. Now Nicole could see that the basket was full of canned goods from the food drive. A sign was taped to the basket. It read:

ENJOY PUBLIC SCHOOL, NICOLE!
THESE ARE IN CASE YOU CAN'T
AFFORD TO BUY FOOD, EITHER.

Nicole's face got hot. She wondered how many people had walked by her locker and seen that sign. She snatched it off the basket, crumpled it up, and tossed it into the garbage can. Her hands were shaking.

"Enjoy public school?" Jordan said. "What does that mean?"

Angry tears came into Nicole's eyes. Someone had told Sheila. It had to be one of the Stars. "I'm transferring to Beachside Middle School. There, are you satisfied?"

"When?"

"Wednesday."

"Tomorrow's your last day?" Jordan seemed shocked—and something else. Angry, maybe.

"Yes." Nicole nudged the basket aside and opened her locker. She started dumping her notebooks into her backpack.

"Why didn't you tell us?"

"Because I didn't want Sheila to find out."

"But, Nicole, Rose and I are your friends. We wouldn't have told Sheila."

Nicole shrugged. "I didn't want to take any chances."

Now Jordan truly seemed angry.

"So you're saying you can't trust us?"

"Listen, Jordan—"

Jordan held up one hand. "No thanks. I think I've heard enough!"

★

Nicole was surprised to see Jordan and Rose waiting when she arrived at Country Day around eight-thirty Tuesday morning. Rose held out a present.

"I'm sorry I blew up at you," Jordan said tentatively.

"That's okay." Nicole forced herself to smile as she took the thin, rectangular package.

Part of her hated the fact that her last day at Country Day had arrived so soon. This part felt that every moment at her old school was precious.

But another part of her wished she didn't have to go to school that day. Thanks to Sheila, everyone at Country Day now knew that she was too poor to attend. Nicole didn't know whether to expect sympathy or ridicule from her classmates. She didn't want either.

She pulled the tissue paper off the package, uncovering a notebook with the Country Day seal on the cover.

"That's so you'll remember your old school," Jordan said quietly.

Tears came to Nicole's eyes. "Thanks, you guys."

She steeled herself as the girls walked into the building together. Nicole immediately knew that plenty of people had walked by her locker the day before. Everyone was staring and whispering. Nicole felt as if she were wearing a sign that read PITIFUL POOR PERSON.

How could the Stars have told Sheila she was leaving? They'd promised not to! Nicole felt deeply betrayed.

"I hope Sheila is out sick today," Nicole said to nobody in particular.

"Yeah," Jordan said. "Preferably with something fatal."

Nicole smiled. Jordan was usually so sweet. Hearing her get catty was funny. But Nicole's smile faded a moment later. Sheila and Rory were walking down the hallway, heading their way.

"Look who it is!" Sheila said loudly.

Rory suddenly pretended to be sad. "Nicole, I was so sorry to hear that your mom got fired."

A couple of kids turned around, obviously curious. The hallway had grown quieter. People were listening.

"She wasn't fired," Nicole said.

"Whatever." Sheila shrugged. "Listen, I've been talking to some of the kids here and telling them how tight money is at your house. Everyone wants to help."

Rory pulled an enormous handful of pennies out of her pocket. "We collected these for you."

Nicole felt like taking the coins and shoving them down Rory's throat. Instead she stepped around the two sneering girls and continued down the hallway. Jordan and Rose hurried to keep up.

"Nicole, I'm so sorry," Rose said softly.

Nicole saw that Jordan's dark eyes were filled with sympathy.

"Well, you know what?" Nicole told her friends. "This just makes leaving easier. Because now I realize that Beachside Middle School has one advantage over Country Day. No Sheila McGarth."

chapter 8

NICOLE WAS UP LATE TUESDAY EVENING.

She'd put off packing her room as long as possible. But the movers were coming first thing the next morning. Sorting through her clothes, books, and CDs took Nicole much longer than she'd expected. She'd been at it for an hour when her father poked his head into her room.

"Aren't you finished yet?"

"No."

"Nicholas finished an hour ago."

"Whoopee for him."

Half an hour later, Ms. Smith came upstairs to help. That sped things up, but the job still wasn't finished until almost ten-thirty. When

Nicole finally crawled into bed, she could hear her father and Tyler still working down the hallway.

Nicole felt rotten the next morning. She was sleepy from staying up late. And she was sad about the move. She couldn't believe this was the last time she was going to wake up in her big pink bedroom.

"You're running late," Ms. Smith told her when she wandered into the kitchen. "The boys left for Beachside High ten minutes ago. Don't forget that Beachside Middle School starts half an hour earlier than Country Day."

"I don't care," Nicole muttered.

"What's that, sweetie?"

"Nothing." This was Nicole's last time to eat breakfast in this kitchen, and she wasn't in any mood to rush. She opened the cereal cabinet. It was empty. Everything was packed.

"What am I going to eat?" she demanded.

"Your father picked up some doughnuts," Ms. Smith said. "There's also some juice. Eat fast and then hurry upstairs and get dressed. I'll drop you off at school."

"I don't want a ride," Nicole protested. What if her new classmates saw her mom? Total embarrassment.

Just then a moving van pulled into the driveway. A bunch of men began climbing out.

"Already?" Ms. Smith glanced at her watch as she started toward the door. "I'll just show them around. Let's leave here in five minutes."

Nicole looked around the kitchen. She couldn't find any doughnuts—although she did find an empty bag with some cinnamon sugar in the bottom.

"Thanks a lot, Tyler," she muttered. Her brother's nickname was the Disposal.

Upstairs, Nicole carefully closed the door so that none of the movers would walk in while she was getting dressed. She couldn't find the outfit she'd picked out the night before. *Mom must have packed it,* she thought in horror. *What do I do now?*

She began ripping open boxes. But she couldn't find her jeans and sweats. In the end she was forced to wear the same outfit she'd had on the day before.

"Let's go!" Ms. Smith hollered.

Nicole grabbed her backpack and pounded down the stairs. Seconds later she was belted into her mom's car. They were halfway down the street before Nicole realized she hadn't said goodbye to her house.

Ms. Smith pulled up in front of Beachside

Middle School. The schoolyard was empty. Nicole was fifteen minutes late.

"I can't go in there now," she protested. "They'll probably suspend me for being this late on my first day."

"I'll go in with you and explain," Ms. Smith suggested.

"No!" Nicole said.

But her mother was already opening her car door and getting out. Nicole scrambled out after her. They walked together to the principal's office.

The principal practically fell all over himself welcoming Nicole to the school. He even insisted on giving Ms. Smith a tour.

After seeing the library and the lunchroom, they finally stopped outside a classroom.

"This is your new room!" the principal told Nicole brightly. "Mrs. Keene is one of our most popular teachers."

Mrs. Keene? Nicole thought. "I thought I'd be in Hollinsworth's class," she protested.

The principal looked surprised. "Oh, no. Maybe you can enter the Gifted and Talented class next year. But first we have to see how you do with our curriculum."

Nicole looked at her mother for help.

Ms. Smith didn't seem to be paying attention. "I'd better get back to the movers," she said nervously. "Have a good day, sweetie. I'll pick you up after school."

Nicole shook her head violently. "Really, Mom—that's okay. I can walk."

"I *want* to pick you up," Ms. Smith insisted. "You're going to be going home to the new house. I don't want you to face that alone."

Nicole had always felt sorry for kids whose moms were always hanging around, going on field trips, and picking them up at school. She didn't want her classmates to think her mother didn't have anything better to do.

"*Please* let me walk."

"Don't be silly," Ms. Smith said briskly. "I'll see you at two-forty-five right out front."

★

Tameka was in the middle of taking a math test when she heard the classroom door open. She stopped punching numbers into her calculator long enough to glance up and see Nicole walk in. The principal was with her.

Tameka shook her head and smiled wryly. She glanced across the room at Yasmine, who shot her an amused look. So Nicole wasn't gifted and talented after all. Somehow that made Tameka feel better.

Mrs. Keene got up and hurried over to Nicole and the principal. They whispered for a few seconds. Then the principal left, and Mrs. Keene showed Nicole to a desk in the front row. Nicole waited until the teacher wasn't looking. Then she turned around and waved at Tameka, Yasmine, and Kyoto.

Tameka waved back.

A couple of kids in the class were checking Nicole out. For her first day at public school, she had dressed in a pair of dressy slacks and an expensive-looking sweater. Her straight blond hair was pulled back with a headband.

The look was all wrong for Beachside Middle School, and Nicole seemed to know it. She kept glancing at the kids around her as if they were aliens. Obviously, Nicole hadn't read her guidebook. Tameka decided to do everything possible to make Nicole feel welcome at Beachside Middle School. The poor girl needed help.

Chapter 9

Tess sat with Yardley, Fiona, and Lacey in the Beachside Middle School lunchroom. Her eyes were on the door. She was waiting for Tameka and Yasmine and Kyoto to appear. Nicole had never turned up in her classroom that morning. Tess was almost certain she knew why.

She spotted a familiar figure coming in. "I knew it! There's Tameka—and Nicole is with her!"

"That private-school education must not have been as superior as she thought," Yardley said.

Lacey made a face. "I bet she wishes she never said that."

"But she did," Fiona said.

Tameka, Yasmine, Kyoto, and Nicole joined them at the table.

"Welcome to Beachside Middle!" Fiona said brightly.

"Thanks."

"We're really happy to have another Star at our school," Lacey said.

"Thanks."

Nicole was being polite. But Tess noticed she hadn't said she was happy to be there.

"What do you think of Mrs. Keene?" Kyoto asked.

"She's nice," Nicole said in a tone that made it clear she had more to say.

"But?" Lacey looked amused.

Nicole didn't need any more encouragement. "Her hair! She looks like she hasn't changed her style since 1952 or something."

Yasmine didn't say anything, but Tess saw her frown. The truth was that Mrs. Keene *did* have bad hair. It formed a big bubble around her face and looked as if she shellacked it with hair spray.

But insulting Mrs. Keene was a bad move. During the few weeks since school had started, Kyoto and Yasmine and Tameka had come to love their teacher like a grandmother. The woman actually brought homemade chocolate chip cookies to class.

Tameka diplomatically changed the subject. "How come you were so late this morning?"

"My mom came in with me," Nicole explained. "The principal gave us a little tour of the building. We spent, like, twenty minutes in the library while he showed off the stupid computers."

"We just got those," Fiona said, apparently trying to explain the principal's enthusiasm. "They're super-fast. And they have a really good connection to the Internet."

Nicole took a bite of carrot. "They were fairly recent models," she said, not sounding impressed. "But my mom was appalled when she found out there were only three of them."

"Why? What's the big deal?" Lacey sounded bugged.

Nicole didn't seem to notice that her comments weren't being well received. "Well, something like six hundred kids go to this school. That's one computer for every two hundred kids. At Country Day, we have computers in every classroom. Dozens of them."

"I guess things are a little different at public school," Kyoto said quietly.

"No joke!" Nicole laughed. "The hallways look like they haven't been painted in years. There's no carpeting. And the dismissal bell is way too loud."

Fiona's neck was turning red. "Anything else?"

Nicole wiggled around. "These chairs are so uncomfortable."

Tess couldn't control herself any longer. "Nicole!" she said sharply.

"What?" Nicole was all innocence.

"You're being totally insulting," Tess said.

Nicole looked surprised. "No, I'm not."

Lacey nodded hard. "Yes, you are."

"You come into our school for a few hours and start telling us what's wrong with it," Yardley said.

"It's kind of like putting down someone's neighborhood," Fiona said.

"Or their family," Tameka added softly.

Nicole stared at them silently for a moment. She started to say something but changed her mind. She began to pack up her lunch.

"Hey, Nicole, come on." Tameka stretched out a hand.

Nicole shook it off. She tossed her carrots and half-eaten sandwich into her bag and stood up.

Tameka shot Tess a "Do something" look, but Tess just shrugged. They had only told Nicole the truth.

And now it was too late anyway. Nicole had turned away from the table and begun pushing her way through the lunchroom.

The rest of the Stars looked at each other.

"*That* went well," Fiona joked.

"I think she feels very welcome here," Lacey said.

The two of them laughed uncomfortably.

Tameka looked worried. "Do you guys think I should go after her?" She was half out of her seat already.

Yasmine shook her head. "I'd give her some time to calm down," she said.

"Well . . . okay," Tameka agreed uncertainly.

For a long moment nobody spoke. They poked at their food. Tess felt only the tiniest bit guilty. They had *tried* to be nice to Nicole. But she'd made it nearly impossible.

Tess wondered if Tiffeny Milbrett and Mia Hamm ever got into little fights like this. Somehow she doubted it. Her thoughts turned to the game. Tickets were going on sale the next day. And their big fund-raiser was that afternoon.

"So." Tess took a deep breath. "Let's talk about the car wash."

★

Nicole spent the rest of lunch hanging out in the library. She made no attempt to pay attention in class that afternoon. If her mother didn't care enough about her to send her to a decent school, why should she bother trying to learn anything?

She sat facing front, doodling in the Country Day notebook Jordan and Rose had given her. She missed her old schoolmates. They wouldn't have let her spend lunch staring out the library window.

The classroom activity swirled around her. Nicole noticed some things about her new surroundings. For example, Mrs. Keene was really into creative writing. At one point during the afternoon, she read a story one of the kids in the class had written. Nicole had a hard time believing this was the work of someone her own age. She felt herself being drawn in—but she resisted. She went back to her doodling and tried not to listen.

About an hour after lunch, the girl behind her tossed a piece of paper onto Nicole's desk.

Nicole immediately covered the paper with her hand to hide it from Mrs. Keene. She picked it up and examined it under her crummy, battered desk.

The paper had been folded over and over until it was less than an inch square.

Probably a note from Tameka, Nicole thought. *An apology.*

Nicole wouldn't let herself turn around to see if Tameka was looking her direction. She slipped the paper into her pants pocket without reading it.

★

An hour later, Nicole stood on the sidewalk outside Beachside Middle School and glanced impatiently at her watch. This awful day had been endless. And now her mother was ten minutes late in picking her up.

She'd hidden in the bathroom until Tess, Tameka, and Yasmine had left the building. But she was nervous about seeing the other Stars. After the way they had treated her at lunch, she planned to avoid them as much as possible. And besides, one of them had told Sheila that she was leaving Country Day. Until she knew which one, she wouldn't trust any of them.

Nicole heard a familiar laugh. She turned around and saw Lacey and Fiona coming out of the building. They were heading her way. Nicole pretended she hadn't seen them. She started to walk toward the corner.

"Nicole!" Fiona called.

"Hey, Nicole!" Lacey chimed in.

Now Nicole pretended not to *hear* them. She walked faster and got to the corner just as a city bus was pulling up. Nicole climbed the steps quickly. She got her wallet out of her backpack and paid the fare. None of the seats was empty, so she grabbed the overhead bar.

The bus was making its first turn when Nicole saw her mother's blue sedan pull up in front of the school. Her mother was going to be worried when she couldn't find Nicole. *Well, too bad,* Nicole thought. *Let her worry.*

Nicole knew this bus route. It was the one she took to get to Geena's house, although she generally got on about five stops later.

Suddenly Nicole was glad that she'd jumped on board. She had an overwhelming desire to see her best friend. Geena would understand how she was feeling. She always did.

Tess, Tameka, Kyoto, and Yasmine ran all the way to the Thomases' and got there only ten minutes after school let out. It was almost three o'clock. They had no time to waste.

They immediately went down to the basement and collected buckets and sponges and rags. By the time they had hauled everything outside, Yardley and Fiona had arrived. Lacey got there about thirty seconds later.

The car wash was under way!

CHAPTER 10

GEENA FELT HARRIED WHEN SHE GOT HOME from school that afternoon. She was already late for the car wash. Even worse: She had to take Luca, her four-and-a-half-year-old brother, with her.

Luca wouldn't leave the house until he had a snack. Geena made him a peanut butter and jelly sandwich. Then she gathered up some cleaning supplies and dumped them into a bag.

By the time she and Luca started walking, it was almost three-thirty. Geena was impatient to get to Tess's house.

They'd made it halfway down the block before Geena spotted Nicole coming the other way. Great.

Maybe Nicole had changed her mind about helping out. She stopped next to her friend.

"Hi," Geena said.

"Hi, Nicole!" Luca said.

"Hi. Where are you going?" Nicole sounded annoyed, as if she expected Geena to stay at home just in case she decided to stop by.

Geena could see that Nicole was upset. Her face was long, and her eyes looked sad. Nicole's first day at Beachside Middle School must not have been a big success.

"We're heading to Tess's," Geena said. "Want to change your mind and come?"

"No." Nicole made a face. "I'm avoiding Tess. And Tameka. And all the other Stars who go to Beachside Middle School."

Geena resisted the urge to groan. Obviously this conversation was going to take some time. She sat down on the curb. Nicole and Luca joined her. Geena knew that Luca would be bored soon. She had only a few minutes to talk.

"So what happened?" Geena asked.

"I *hate* Beachside Middle School," Nicole said with great feeling. "The place is *so* depressing. The halls are gray. The paint is peeling off the ceiling. Someone scribbled on the top of my desk—*which* is in the front row right next to the teacher. Oh, and the lunchroom smells like dirty socks."

Geena laughed. "Anything else? Don't hold back on my account."

"It's not funny!" Nicole said loudly.

Geena watched Luca run his feet through the leaves in the gutter. He was humming quietly to himself.

"The place deserves to be condemned," Nicole added.

Geena didn't know what to say. She knew Nicole was exaggerating. None of the other Stars ever complained about Beachside Middle School. She'd heard them talk about their teachers and classes, and it seemed as if they were learning the same stuff she was.

"Wasn't there *anything* you liked?"

"Actually, no."

Luca stood up. "Can we go now? I'm bored."

"In just one minute." Geena gave him a pleading look.

Luca sighed and slumped down again. He pulled up a blade of grass and tried to use it to make a whistle between his thumbs.

"Did you eat lunch with any of the Stars?" Geena asked.

"I tried, but they were so mean! Tess got all mad just because I said the library didn't have enough computers."

Geena could imagine what Nicole had *really* said. "Well, I'm sure things will be better tomorrow," she ventured. "Maybe if you apologize—"

"Apologize? For what? I didn't do anything. And trust me, things aren't going to get better. Not unless my parents send me back to Country Day."

"Is that possible?"

"Sure. My mom would just have to get a real job again."

"Nicole! That is so selfish."

"It is not!"

"Yes, it is! The only person you ever think about is yourself. Haven't you ever thought about all the people your mother could help at the free clinic?"

"I don't care about them."

"That's the problem!"

Geena stood up. She'd heard enough. Sometimes she couldn't understand how Nicole could be so self-centered. She reached for Luca's hand. "Let's go."

"Where are you going? I need you to help me

figure out a way to convince my parents to send me back to Country Day."

"I don't want to help you."

"Why not?"

"Because I agree with your mom. Sending you to the most expensive school in town is not the most important thing in the world. So far it seems like all you've learned there is how to act like a spoiled brat."

★

Nicole watched Geena and Luca walk away. She couldn't believe that Geena had called her selfish. And a brat! Obviously she'd been wrong about Geena. The girl didn't have a sympathetic bone in her body.

Geena was the one who was selfish. She couldn't spare a moment for her best friend. No, she was too busy rushing off to the stupid car wash.

Nicole could imagine all the Stars washing cars and laughing, and that made her feel lonelier. She reminded herself that the Stars weren't her friends. Friends kept secrets when you asked them to.

The bus pulled up on the street Nicole was facing, and she began to run for it. Since she had nothing else to do, she felt a sudden urge to get over to the new house fast. She was hungry. She had eaten only half of her lunch.

★

Tess looked around the Thomases' yard and smiled. All the Stars had shown up, except for Nicole. They were hard at work.

Fiona and Lacey were rinsing off a dark blue Mazda that was pulled into Tameka's driveway.

Geena was crawling around inside the car, vacuuming. Her little brother Luca had pulled the mats out from under the seat. He was scrubbing them on the driveway. Rory was doing the windows from the inside. And Sheila was working on the windows from the outside.

The car's owner, a glamorous woman with bleached blond hair and oversized sunglasses, was sitting in the Thomases' yard on one of the lawn chairs they'd set out for their customers.

The chairs were Geena's idea. She'd also suggested they provide a stack of magazines to keep their customers happy while they waited. Tameka had added her own touch—a pitcher of water and some glasses.

The rest of the team was finishing up an old Honda that had pulled to the curb. The owner was an elderly man who wore a green fishing hat. Mr. Thomas was chatting with him about soccer. While Tess watched, the old gentleman pulled out a ten-dollar bill and handed it to Yasmine.

Tess hurried over to get it. The girls had decided that one person should collect all the money. That way they wouldn't get distracted and forget to charge someone.

"Thank you!" Tess said. She'd already collected forty dollars. *We're going to have enough money in no time,* she thought.

★

Nicole didn't get home until almost four o'clock. But the long bus ride had given her plenty of time to think. She'd made up her mind. She was going to demand that her parents send her back to Country Day.

She let herself in through her new kitchen door, feeling as if she were trespassing. The place was a mess. Every cabinet door was open. The counters and floor were covered with boxes neatly marked KITCHEN—DISHES in her mother's handwriting.

Nicole was pulling a yogurt out of the refrigerator when her mother came into the kitchen. She looked tired. She was wearing jeans and a faded

T-shirt that read NORTHWESTERN UNIVERSITY LAW SCHOOL.

"Hello, Nicole." Ms. Smith's voice was cool.

"Hi, Mom. Listen, we have to talk."

"I'll say! Where were you this afternoon? I left in the middle of the move, drove over there, and waited for half an hour." Ms. Smith had her hands on her hips. She didn't look tired anymore. Now she looked angry.

Nicole blinked in surprise. She'd forgotten that she had blown off her mother that afternoon. She started to explain. "You were late, so I—"

"You left!"

Nicole stared at her mother's angry face, feeling terribly mistreated. How could her mother yell at her *now*? Why didn't she ask about Nicole's first day at a new school?

Because she doesn't care about me, Nicole thought. *All she cares about is herself.*

Part of Nicole knew this wasn't true. This part said that if she had met her mother as she'd promised, her mother would have asked her plenty of questions about school.

But Nicole wasn't in the mood to think rationally. She felt as if she had spent the entire day getting yelled at. And she was sick of it.

"That's right, I left," she said. "And I'm going to do it again!"

Nicole slammed her uneaten yogurt down on the counter. She marched out of the kitchen.

"Young lady, you come back here!" Ms. Smith ordered.

Nicole kept going. She went up the stairs to her tiny new room. She tossed her new schoolbooks out of her backpack onto the floor. She opened boxes until she found some underwear and her favorite fleecy sweatshirt.

She was fed up with being bossed around. When she had her things together, she walked down the steps and straight out the front door. She didn't bother to tell her mother she was leaving home forever.

In fact, the idea that she was running away from home was ridiculous. Her parents had sold her home. And they hadn't even asked her how she felt about it.

chapter 11

A LITTLE AFTER FOUR O'CLOCK, THINGS AT the car wash started to get busy.

Several of the Stars' parents stopped by. A few teachers. And Marina, the girls' former coach, pulled up in an old powder blue Beetle she'd just bought.

Tess worked on almost every car that pulled in. She filled an entire garbage bag with old fast-food boxes she pulled out of some college kid's car. He gave her a quarter tip.

She washed the perfectly clean windows on a Mercedes that belonged to Rory's mom. The thing was beautiful—red with real leather seats. Mrs. Carver said they could keep any change they found in the car. Total take: $4.61.

Some lady drove up in a minivan with a four-year-old and two-year-old twins. Tess vacuumed up Cheerios while Yasmine wiped apple-juice spills out of the cup holders. Sheila was working on the insides of the windows. Rory was doing the outsides.

"So Nicole isn't going to show up, huh?" Sheila asked.

"I doubt it," Tess said. "We . . . sort of had a little argument at school today."

Sheila raised her eyebrows. "An argument? About what?"

"Well . . ." Tess felt creepy discussing Nicole with Sheila. She knew they didn't get along. "Nothing important," she finished uneasily.

"Let's just say Nicole's first day at Beachside Middle School didn't go that smoothly," Yasmine put in.

Sheila smiled as she sprayed window cleaner on a side window. "I bet it was better than her last day at Country Day." She sounded pleased with herself.

"Why? What happened?" Tess asked.

"Oh . . . nothing, really." Sheila's expression was smug. "Let's just say I gave her a little going-away present."

Tess and Yasmine exchanged worried looks.

"How did you know she was leaving?" Yasmine asked.

"Your brother told me," Sheila said. "And if you get a chance, thank him for me. That little bit of information really made my week."

"Yeah . . . ," Yasmine said. "I'll definitely talk to him about it."

Tess could tell Yasmine was upset with Yago. She could imagine the "talk" they'd have.

The Stars finished up the minivan. By then it was after five and getting dark.

"I think it's time to close up shop, girls," Mr. Thomas called from the porch.

Tess agreed. She was tired. She flopped down in one of the lawn chairs and watched Yasmine, Lacey, and Tameka finish up the last car. She felt completely satisfied. The car wash had been a much bigger success than she could have imagined.

Tameka ran inside, came out with a carton of sodas, and started passing them around. Sheila sat down in the other chair. Everyone else stretched out on the grass around them. Luca plopped into Geena's lap. He had grass in his hair.

"So how did we do?" Lacey asked.

Tess pulled a wad of bills and a handful of coins

out of her jeans. "I'll count our earnings." She put the change down on the table. She smoothed out the paper money and started sorting it into ones, fives, tens, and twenties.

"Am I going to get paid?" Luca demanded. "I worked hard too!"

"Well . . ." Tess looked to Geena for help.

"Of course," Geena said. "Why don't you keep all the pennies?"

Luca beamed. "Thanks!"

Tess started to count.

"This was fun," Lacey said.

"We should do it once a week after games," Kyoto said. "We'd be rich."

Tess finished counting. She felt her heart skip a beat. *I must have counted wrong,* she thought. She started over again but got the same result. This time when she finished, she noticed that Tameka was staring at her.

"What's the matter?" Tameka asked.

"We have a problem," Tess said.

★

Nicole was angry. She wanted to get as far away from her mother as possible. She walked fast. Down grungy little Gray Lane with its ugly brick sidewalk. Past the barns on Beach Street. By the shops on North Lake, around the annoying shoppers who stood in the middle of the sidewalk, and all the way down to the playing fields.

It was late Wednesday afternoon, and the fields were deserted. Nicole walked through the empty parking lot, past the locked-up rest rooms, and onto the grass. She sat down right on the center line and thought angry thoughts.

Why didn't the Stars understand what she was going through? She had to move and change schools, and they expected her to be nice. They wanted her to smile. Well, she didn't feel like smiling or being nice. She felt like yelling and pouting and hiding under her covers.

Nicole told herself she didn't care what the Stars thought. Who needed them? Especially since they couldn't even keep a secret from stupid Sheila McGarth. If she could leave home, she could leave the Stars too. They'd be sorry when she never, ever showed up at another game again. They'd wish they'd been more understanding.

The sun was going down, and the temperature was dropping. Nicole got out her sweatshirt and pulled it on. She went back to the sidewalk and started walking again, still heading away from home.

It would be dinnertime soon. Nicole could imagine what was happening at her house: Her mother was in the messy kitchen. She was making what she always made when she was too busy to cook a real dinner—chocolate chip pancakes.

She'd call Nicole. Then call again more loudly. No answer.

Her mother would climb the steps and look in Nicole's new room. Empty. She'd walk through the house again, calling Nicole's name. She'd think about the fight they'd had and start getting nervous.

The rest of the family would join the search. Nicole's brothers would walk up and down the streets. "Nicole! Nicole, please come home!" they'd call.

Nicole's mom would call her dad at the office. He'd phone the police. Lacey's dad would come. The whole neighborhood would join in the search. All the Stars would be there. They'd search and search but never find her. Nicole's mother would blame herself. She'd be unable to sleep, to work—to do anything but worry about her precious baby.

A car beeped at Nicole and startled her. She looked over at the street, but it wasn't anyone she knew. She quickly turned away, feeling slightly threatened. Had the driver really been beeping at *her?* Or just at another car? Nicole wasn't sure, but it was creepy anyway.

The street had widened, and traffic moved faster. Nobody else was on the sidewalk. Nicole passed a big office building. Some lights were on, and she could see the deserted desks and chairs inside. The place seemed completely empty.

She passed the office building's parking lot. It was dimly lit, and Nicole walked faster. Only one car was parked on the entire acre of asphalt. And the motor was running.

Nicole hurried by. Next came a car dealership. It too was deserted. She passed a long line of cars with price stickers on their windshields. They were all the same model but different colors. It occurred to Nicole that someone could easily hide in any of those cars. All they'd have to do is crouch down in the front seat, then jump out and grab her.

Her heart was racing, and she had to fight an urge to run. She thought about turning back toward more familiar territory. But that would mean walking past all those cars again. Nicole didn't have the nerve.

She kept going, heading toward a highway overpass. At the corner, she hesitated. She wasn't sure which way to turn. She had two choices: Keep going straight, or turn right and cross four lanes of traffic. On the other side of the road, the sidewalk curved out of sight.

While Nicole was trying to decide, a woman suddenly appeared beside her. She had a big dog on a leash. The woman gave Nicole a curious glance. Then the Walk light changed and the woman moved across the street.

Nicole followed her. She felt safer with another person, even a stranger. But a few blocks later the woman went into an apartment building.

The street Nicole was on now was lined with three-story brick buildings. People were hanging around on the sidewalk. Three young women stood chatting in front of a store that had fruit displayed outside. A couple were looking into the window of a shop that sold unfinished furniture.

Nicole knew she looked out of place. She was the only kid on the street, and she didn't want anyone asking her questions. She kept her eyes down.

Up ahead was some sort of restaurant. A group of people was standing outside, laughing loudly.

Nicole froze. One of the people—a big man— was looking at her.

His long gray hair was tied back into a ponytail. He was wearing ratty jeans, a black T-shirt, and heavy biker's boots. Nicole was afraid to walk past him. He looked dangerous—like someone who might attack her.

The man leaned over and whispered something to one of his friends. They started toward Nicole.

Nicole turned and fled. She darted around the couple looking at furniture and turned left at the first intersection. Her brand-new gym shoes pounded on the broken pavement. She ran by quiet houses with dark lawns, praying for a gas station or a fast-food restaurant. Any place brightly lit and crowded.

She passed a woman watering her lawn but didn't slow down. Her lungs and thighs ached, but she kept going. Maybe at the end of this block she'd find a main street. Or a police station. Or anything that looked familiar.

Finally Nicole couldn't run anymore. She stopped and looked behind her. Nobody was there. She put her hands on her knees and sobbed with relief. As soon as she caught her breath, she started walking again.

Still, Nicole felt jumpy. She kept glancing over her shoulder to see if anyone was hiding in the shadows. She realized there was no way she could spend the night outside. Maybe running away wasn't such a great idea. . . .

She decided to find a phone booth and call home. Her mom or dad would come and pick her up. She might get in trouble. But that was better than getting attacked by some hippie biker.

Nicole walked and walked without seeing a phone booth. The street here was narrower and lined with apartment buildings. Nicole was afraid to ask any of the people she saw where she might find a phone. She didn't want anyone to know she was lost and feeling helpless.

Finally she saw a familiar city bus-stop sign. Underneath was an old bench, and it was empty. Nicole couldn't resist. She had blisters on both heels, and her legs ached. She sat down at the bus stop and waited. She didn't even care where the bus was going. Anywhere was better than here.

chapter 12

KYOTO WAS RIDING HARD. IT WAS PAST dark, and her father hated for her to be out past dark. Two more blocks and she'd be home. She was looking forward to dinner. After three hours washing cars, she was hungry.

She turned the corner onto Harrison Avenue and bumped her bike up onto the sidewalk. Harrison was on a slight hill, and Kyoto got up off her seat so that she could pedal harder.

The bike was just picking up speed when Kyoto passed the bus stop. She saw Nicole sitting there and started to wave before she realized how strange this was. She hit the brakes, then put her feet down and turned around.

"Nicole?"

Nicole looked up and broke into a radiant grin. "Kyoto! What are you doing here?"

"Going home," Kyoto said. She could see that something was wrong with Nicole. Her eyes were red and puffy, as if she'd been crying. Her hair was sticking out funny. And she seemed way too happy to see Kyoto.

"What are *you* doing *here*?" Kyoto asked. She'd never seen Nicole on the south side before.

She'd heard that Nicole was moving. But Fiona had said that Nicole's new house was in the fancy historic part of town. North Lake Street, around that area.

Nicole's eyes darted around nervously. She got up off the bench and came to stand next to Kyoto and her bike. "I—well, I'm lost."

"Where are you trying to go?"

For some reason this made Nicole burst into tears. "I don't know! I had to get away from my mom and I just started walking and ended up here."

"Hard day, huh?"

"Yes . . ." Nicole's cheeks suddenly colored, and Kyoto guessed she had just remembered what had happened at lunch.

Well, Kyoto wasn't about to bring that up. She could tell that Nicole was freaked out, and she wanted to help.

"Have you eaten dinner yet?" Kyoto asked.

"No. And I just realized that I'm starving." Nicole laughed uneasily. "I missed most of lunch too."

Kyoto smiled tentatively, glad that Nicole was laughing about it. "Why don't you come to my place?" she offered. "We'll share whatever Dad has on the stove."

"Thanks!" Nicole sounded as if she'd just been saved from drowning.

"Climb on."

Nicole hesitated for a second. Then she swung her leg over the seat and made herself as comfortable as possible.

Kyoto pushed off, heading for home.

Nicole couldn't believe her good luck. She had to fight an urge to hug Kyoto. Being with someone she knew and trusted felt incredibly good.

She relaxed as Kyoto steered through the darkened streets. Getting out of this neighborhood was going to feel good too. Nicole was startled when Kyoto took a quick right into a large driveway.

"Where are we going?" Nicole demanded. She wasn't in the mood for any stops. She wanted to go straight to Kyoto's house—wherever that was.

"Home," Kyoto said simply. She coasted up to a high chain-link fence and put her feet down. "Could you get off, please?"

Nicole got off the bike, staring up at the building. Kyoto lived here?

The apartment house was old and at least three stories tall. Light shone out of some of the windows. Nicole could see books lined up on some windowsills, plants on others. Hip-hop music spilled out of an apartment on the second floor. A baby was crying somewhere else.

All Nicole's anxiety flooded back. She was still in foreign territory. Nicole didn't see any way out of going upstairs now. She crossed her fingers and prayed that the apartment wouldn't be too awful. She hoped there would be a phone, at least.

Kyoto fiddled with her bike lock for a long time. Finally she stood up and smiled at Nicole. "Follow me," she said.

Nicole followed.

Kyoto had to use a key to open the door from the street. They walked up some stairs and past a row of metal mailboxes. Nicole could smell curry, and it made her mouth water.

Three more flights of stairs and a left turn. Kyoto stopped in front of apartment 15 and unlocked the door. "Daddy! I'm home!"

Nicole stepped inside in time to see Kyoto's father get up off the couch. He gave Kyoto a sideways hug. "It's late," he said gently. "What kept you so long?"

"The car wash took forever! Daddy, this is my friend Nicole. She's hungry and needs to use the phone."

Kyoto's father came forward and took Nicole's hand. "Nice to meet you, Nicole."

"Thank you. Nice to meet you too."

He was a slim man wearing tan trousers and a neat green sweater. His face was deeply lined, and his hair was sprinkled with gray.

"I'll get the food," he said.

"I'll set another place," Kyoto said. "Nicole, do you want to wash your hands? The bathroom is right in there." She pointed.

"Thanks." Nicole stepped into the tight space and closed the door. The tiny room seemed to be the only bathroom in the apartment. Nicole had her own bathroom—even in the new house.

Nicole washed her hands, feeling very sorry for Kyoto. She wondered if she should tell the other Stars how Kyoto lived. Maybe they could do something to help.

When Nicole came out of the bathroom, the food was on the table. Two places had been set, each with a big portion of steaming rice, a hamburger patty, and lots of spinach and carrots.

"Sit down," Kyoto's dad said with a smile.

Nicole sat down, noticing that each chair around the table was different. How embarrassing! Even the silverware was mismatched.

Kyoto sat down and picked up her fork. "Enjoy," she said.

For the next five minutes Nicole concentrated on eating. The food was plain, but she was too hungry to care. In fact, it tasted delicious.

Kyoto chatted with her dad about his day, and Nicole discovered that he was a gardener. No wonder they didn't live in a fancy house! Nicole noticed that Kyoto asked her father lots of questions about the different people he worked for. She didn't seem embarrassed that he was basically a servant.

In fact, Nicole was slowly starting to realize, Kyoto didn't seemed embarrassed by her home either. She was smiling and seemed relaxed. And she hadn't hesitated for a second before inviting Nicole over.

"I'm very glad to have met you," Kyoto's father said as they cleared the table. "I always enjoy having Kyoto's friends over to dinner."

"Oh." Nicole was surprised. "Who else has come?"

Kyoto shrugged. "Tess and Lacey."

Nicole couldn't believe this. Tess and Lacey had been here, and they hadn't told the rest of the team that Kyoto lived on the south side? In an *apartment* building?

Something else hit her like a goal kick to the stomach: Tess and Lacey both liked Kyoto. Better than they liked Nicole, even. And they had seen her home.

Maybe having to move isn't such a big deal, Nicole realized. She still wasn't thrilled with Beachside Middle School. But she had to admit that Kyoto was a much better classmate than Sheila.

"Want some ice cream?" Kyoto offered.

"What kind?"

"Green tea."

"Um—no thanks. But could I use your phone? My parents are probably worried about me."

"Sure."

Kyoto showed Nicole into a back bedroom.

Nicole sat down in an old wicker chair and dialed her home number. Her mom picked up on the first ring.

"Hi, Mom. It's me."

"Nicole! Where have you been? We're all worried silly."

"I, um . . . needed some time to think."

"Think *where*?"

"I'm at a friend's apartment," Nicole said. She gave her mother the address.

"I'll be right over," Ms. Smith said.

Nicole hung up the phone and walked back into the kitchen. Kyoto had already finished washing the dishes. She was setting her schoolbooks out on the kitchen table. Her father was sitting on the couch, reading a Japanese newspaper.

"My mom is on her way," Nicole announced.

"Is she mad?" Kyoto whispered.

"A little."

Kyoto made a sympathetic face. "Come on. We can wait for her on the stoop. That way she won't have to get out of her car and ring the doorbell."

Nicole hesitated. "Is that safe?"

"Sure," Kyoto said, as if surprised by the question.

The girls went outside and sat on the steps. Nicole wondered what she was going to say to her mother. But thinking about that started to make her too nervous. She turned to Kyoto. "So. How did the car wash go?"

Kyoto sighed and looked sad. "It was fun. And at first we thought it went very well. But we didn't make all the money we needed. We're seventy dollars short. Everyone is really upset."

"So what's the plan?" Nicole asked.

"We're thinking about opening the car wash again tomorrow," Kyoto said. "The only problem is that we'll have to wait until Friday morning to order the tickets and they might be sold out by then. We rushed the car wash so Mrs. Adams could order tickets as soon as they go on sale tomorrow. The only other option is paying the difference ourselves."

Something in Kyoto's tone made Nicole look at her face.

Kyoto's eyes were on the ground and she wouldn't meet Nicole's gaze.

Something clicked in Nicole's brain. Kyoto *couldn't* pay. That was why Tess had suddenly gotten so excited about raising the money.

Nicole made a decision. "I can't go to the game, anyway," she said. "I don't have the cash. . . ." She almost added "either," but chickened out at the last moment. What if she was wrong about Kyoto's situation?

Kyoto looked up, her expression shocked. "You don't?"

Nicole shook her head. "Ever since my mom quit her job, she's been totally stingy. I get my allowance and that's it."

Kyoto smiled sadly. "We might be the only Stars who can't go to the game. Maybe we should spend that afternoon together."

"Sure," Nicole agreed. "We can watch the game on TV at my house. It's going to be on ESPN 2."

Kyoto's expression changed. "Let me get this straight," she said, sounding amused. "Your mom is pinching pennies—but you still have premium cable?"

"Well . . . yeah."

Now Kyoto was grinning. "That's the kind of stingy I could get into!"

chapter 13

Ms. Smith's car rolled down Kyoto's street. Nicole quickly jumped up and thanked Kyoto for dinner. She got into the car. She didn't feel threatened in this neighborhood anymore. But she was still glad she didn't live here.

"Explain," Ms. Smith said as she drove.

"I was running away from home," Nicole said sullenly. "This is as far as I got."

Ms. Smith took her eyes off the road long enough to stare at Nicole. "Why were you running away?"

The question bugged Nicole. Was her mother completely clueless?

"Mom, have you totally forgotten what it's like to be a kid?" she asked. "Moving is practically the end of the world. And changing schools is even worse! You dropped both nasty little events on me in one day. And you never even asked if I minded."

"Well, I . . ." Ms. Smith ran out of words and frowned. She was quiet for several blocks.

Nicole stared out the window, waiting to hear what her mom would say.

Finally Ms. Smith sighed. "You know, Nicole, you're not the first person to tell me something like that."

"I'm not?"

"Nope. See, I tend to get so focused on what I want that I forget my actions affect other people. Starting up this clinic is a big project. And I've been attacking it head-on. I guess I forgot about you kids in the process."

"I guess so."

"Can I do anything to make it up to you?"

Nicole thought about that. Maybe she could ask to go back to Country Day. But when Nicole thought about her old school now, the first image that popped into her mind was Sheila's smirking face. Going to a school where she didn't have any enemies might be a good change. And Mrs. Keene *did* seem nice.

"Can we move back to the house?" Nicole asked.

Ms. Smith sighed. "Honey, we can't. And that place is too big for us anyway. I think you'll really like Gray Lane once you give it a chance."

"Maybe." Fiona and Yardley *did* live nearby. Of course, they had told her secret to Sheila, for all Nicole knew.

Ms. Smith snapped her fingers as she pulled into the drive. "I almost forgot! A boy called for you." She sounded both worried and pleased.

"A boy? Did he leave a message?"

"Yes. He said his name was Yale Madrigal."

"Yago?"

"That's it!"

"Yago Madrigal called *me*?" Nicole's voice was squeaky.

Ms. Smith nodded as she pulled the car into their new driveway. "He said he needed to talk to you right away."

★

Yasmine paced impatiently. It was almost bedtime, and Nicole still hadn't returned Yago's call. She *had* to be home by now.

The noise of Yago's favorite video game came from the family room. Yasmine walked in. Her brother was seated on the edge of the couch, zapping away.

"Call her again," Yasmine demanded.

"Get real." Yago's eye hadn't left the screen. "I said I'd call her once and I did. My job here is finished."

"Do it, garlic breath."

"Or what?"

Yasmine considered. "Or I'll tell Mom about the time you wrote the answers to that math test on your hand."

"And I'll tell her you skipped school."

"I did not!"

Yago shrugged. *Zap, zap, zap.* "I'll still tell her."

Yasmine groaned in frustration. She'd had enough of Yago. She marched to the phone and punched in Nicole's number.

"Hello?"

"Nicole, hi! It's Yasmine."

"Oh, hi." Nicole's voice was suddenly cool.

"Listen, Sheila let something incredible drop at the car wash today. Yago told her you were leaving Country Day—way back on Saturday. While we were all at Regina's."

"And how did he know?" Nicole still sounded angry.

"Because he was there when Mom told me," Yasmine explained. "Listen, I'm really sorry I didn't think about this earlier. I should have told him to keep his big mouth shut. Did Sheila make your life miserable?"

"Definitely."

"I'm sorry."

Nicole didn't say anything for a moment. Then she sighed. "Don't sweat it," she said. "And . . . and well, I'm sorry if I put down Beachside Middle at lunch today. I didn't mean to upset you guys."

Yasmine was surprised. Nicole was saying she was sorry. This was unprecedented. "Don't sweat it," she said with a smile.

★

Nicole hung up the phone. So the Stars hadn't told Sheila her secret after all. Suddenly Nicole felt guilty about suspecting her teammates. And she wished she hadn't missed the car wash. Maybe if she'd pitched in, they could have washed more cars and raised all the money they needed.

She looked around her new kitchen. The glass-fronted cabinets were still empty. Cardboard boxes sat on the floor and counters. A few had been opened. Dirty dishes were stacked in the sink.

Ms. Smith had offered to pay Nicole to pack up the kitchen in the old house. Nicole wondered if her mother would pay her the same amount to *unpack* at the new house. If she did, Nicole would have enough money to pay for a ticket.

But what about Kyoto? Nicole couldn't go to the game and leave Kyoto home.

I could buy two cheap seats with that twenty-five dollars, Nicole thought. That way she and Kyoto could both go to the game. The only problem was that they wouldn't be able to sit with the rest of the Stars. Of course, *that* would only be a problem if the Stars scraped up enough money to go.

An idea hit Nicole. She rushed over to the wall phone and dialed Tess's number.

"Hello?" Tess sounded sad.

"Hi, Tess. It's Nicole. Listen, I heard about the car wash—"

"We're all so bummed out," Tess interrupted. "It looks like we'll have to wait until Friday to order the tickets—*if* we have enough money by then."

"You have enough money now," Nicole said.

"How's that?"

"Order the cheap seats!" Nicole said triumphantly.

Tess gasped. "I forgot! All my calculations were based on the good seats. The cheap ones are only ten dollars!"

"I know," Nicole said with satisfaction.

"Should I order a ticket for you?" Tess asked. "We'll have enough money now."

"Well . . ." Nicole was tempted. But she didn't feel right saying yes. After all, she hadn't helped out with the car wash. "I think I'd rather pay my own way," she said.

"Whatever."

The girls talked a few minutes longer. When they hung up, Nicole went looking for her mother. She had to talk to her about those dishes.

★

Tess was applauding so hard that her hands stung. It was Saturday of Thanksgiving weekend, and all eleven Stars were lined up in the cheap seats at Soldier Field. Rory's dad was there with them. So was Yasmine's mom.

The U.S. Women's National Team had just jogged onto the field. Tess stood up and clapped even harder. She knew them all by their numbers. The attackers were Mia Hamm, Michelle Akers, and Tiffeny Milbrett.

Tess had been too excited to sleep the night before. Nothing in the world made her happier than seeing this team play. Well, except maybe for playing herself.

"This is going to be beautiful," Tess told Tameka, who was sitting next to her.

Tameka nodded.

Tess moved to the front of her seat as the game got under way. The United States was playing Germany—another one of the best teams in women's soccer.

The American team had the kickoff, and the attackers immediately began putting the pressure on. Germany's defense responded well. The ball was in constant motion, although it rarely moved into U.S. territory. Tess couldn't believe the control these women had. Even the defenders seemed to aim precisely.

"Nobody is out of position," Tess commented.

"I don't know how they play on such a big field," Yasmine said. The field was almost half again as big as the ones the Stars played on.

"They're in better shape than we are," Tess said without removing her eyes from the field. She could imagine how tired she'd get running all those extra steps. She vowed to start jogging every day after school.

In the sixteenth minute, Mia Hamm took the ball out of the air, turned with the grace of a ballet dancer, and buried it deep in the net.

"Yes!" Tess, Tameka, and Yasmine jumped to their feet. They shouted their approval along with the rest of the crowd.

The ball was centered quickly. The Americans continued to attack. Mia and Michelle got close to scoring more than once. But now the German attackers were getting into the game. They got off several shots that made Tess gasp in fear. Amazingly, the U.S. goalkeeper, Briana Scurry, stopped them all.

Thirty-nine minutes in, Mia Hamm scored again. Tess was practically bouncing in her seat. The score was 2 to 0.

"We've got a comfortable lead," Tess said happily.

That lasted about two minutes. A fast-footed German attacker named Prinz scored just before the halftime whistle.

"Forty-five minutes in one *half*," Yasmine said as Tess watched the players trot off the field. "Our game would almost be over."

"They're amazing," Tess said happily.

Yardley touched her arm. "All this cheering is making me hungry. Come on, let's get a hot dog or something."

Tess shook her head. "I'll stay here."

She could imagine how long the lines at the concession stands would be. She didn't want to risk missing any of the game for a *hot dog*.

"I'll bring you something back," Tameka promised.

The Stars filed out, talking excitedly. Tess sat in the stands alone and promised herself she'd be a member of this team someday. Watching the women play had only made her more determined.

Tameka and the others came back just as the game was getting under way again. Once more the United States started fast and came close to scoring. But the German goalkeeper was tough.

About twelve minutes into the second half, the ref called a foul on the Germans. Tiffeny Milbrett set up and took the free kick so fast that Tess almost missed it. Again the German goalkeeper stopped the ball from going in. Tess hoped Kyoto was watching her moves.

Now the Germans began to dominate the play. Tess's heart was in her throat as they shot again and again. But Briana Scurry rose to the challenge.

Finally, late in the second half, Tiffeny Milbrett took the ball into Germany's territory. She sent a blistering pass to the middle. Mia Hamm ran to the ball and bounced it in.

"That makes a hat trick!" Tess shouted happily.

"A what?" Yardley was looking at her as if she were crazy.

"Three goals in one glorious game!" Tess told her. "Mia is the greatest."

Tess felt a strange mixture of emotions as time ran out. She was still elated from watching the game. But she was also disappointed that it was over.

As the Stars made their way out, Nicole fell into step next to her. "Thanks for organizing this. That was the best game I've ever seen."

"Even though we had to sit in the cheap seats?" Tess couldn't resist teasing Nicole a little.

Nicole stuck her tongue out. "Where you sit doesn't matter," she said. "What's important is being with your friends."

Soccer Tips from AYSO

BECOMING A COMPLETE ATTACKING PLAYER

It's important to remember when you're playing in the attacking third of the field that your primary objective is to score.

Everyone remembers the perfect shot that frames the upper right corner of the goal and beats a diving goalkeeper, but many games are won by a player who has the ability to put errant shots and rebounded balls into the back of the net. It might take the inside of your left or right foot, even your chest, or your head to put the ball in the net. What's important is that the ball goes into the back of the net. All coaches will stress the importance of good soccer technique; however, players who can put loose balls into the back of the goal using any technique they have are a very important part of the attack. It's more important that the ball goes to the back of the net than how pretty it looks going in.

To score on loose balls, remember two things.

1. You need to follow every shot until the keeper has made the save and releases the ball back into play. Never assume that the goalkeeper is going to make the save just because it was an easy shot. Many funny things can happen in front of the goal. The keeper may be nervous, the

ball may take a bad bounce, the keeper may be unable to see the shot, he or she might just misplay the ball. You need to be in a position to put the missed played ball into the back of the net. Remember, balls also can rebound off the goalpost.

2. Be in position to retrieve loose balls. Learn to read the flight of the ball on the ground and in the air. Reading the flight of the ball will prepare you to read the location you should be trying to get to if the ball is deflected or bounces off the keeper, other players, or the goalpost. Being in the right place at the right time is half the battle. If you aren't in a position to collect loose balls you won't be able to score on loose balls.

Putting loose balls into the back of the net is a skill, so practice it. Scoring is fun—you'll see.

AYSO Soccer Definitions

Attacker: The player in control of the ball, attempting to score a goal. Attackers need speed, power, good ball control, and accurate aim. Sometimes referred to as forward.

AYSO: American Youth Soccer Organization, a nationwide organization guided by five principles:

1. Everyone plays
2. Balanced teams
3. Open registration
4. Positive coaching
5. Good sportsmanship

Cleats: Projections on the soles of soccer shoes that provide support and a good grip on the soccer field.

Defender: The player whose primary duty is to prevent the opposing team from getting a good shot at the goal. Defenders need sufficient speed to cover opposing players, good tackling skills, and determination to win control of the ball.

Direct kick: A penalty kick awarded by the referee when a serious foul has been committed. A goal may be scored by the player taking the direct kick. No other player needs to touch the ball for the goal to be scored.

Dribbling: Moving the ball along the ground by a series of short taps with one or both feet.

Goal: Scored when the entire ball crosses the line between the goalposts and underneath the crossbar. One goal equals one point.

Goalkeeper: The last line of defense. The goalkeeper is the only player who can use her hands during play within the penalty area.

Halftime: A five- to ten-minute break in the middle of a game.

Halfway line: A line that marks the middle of the field.

Indirect kick: A penalty kick awarded by the referee when the foul is less serious. A second player of either team must touch the ball before a goal can be scored.

Midfielder: The player who supports the attack on the goal with accurate passes and hustles to get back to help the defense. Positioned in the middle of the field, she must have stamina for continuous running.

Open: A player who is not being marked or covered by a member of the opposing team is open.

Passing: Kicking the ball to a teammate.

Referee: An official who ensures the safety of all the players by enforcing the rules during a game.

Save: The prevention of an attempted goal, usually by the goalkeeper.

Scrimmage: A practice game.

Short-sided: A short-sided game is played with fewer than eleven players per team.

Substitution break: A quick break during which the coaches can put in new players and the players can grab a sip of water. Substitution breaks come at a quarter and three quarters of the way through a game.

Throw-in: When the ball crosses the touchline, it is thrown back onto the field by a member of the team that did not touch the ball last. The thrower must keep both feet on or behind the touchline and throw the ball over her head.

Touchlines: Out-of-bounds lines that run along the long edges of the field.

Trapping: Gaining control of the ball by using feet, thighs, or chest.